Two days with Angie felt like a gift for him and Carly.

She made life fun and meaningful. And yet a flicker of concern tightened his chest. He had to be careful. He'd already feared her hesitation to plant today was because of something he'd said.

"If we're finishing the planting tomorrow…" She paused and looked at Carly. "We might have time to go the park today."

"The park? Really?" A gleeful giggle escaped Carly. "Can we, Daddy?"

"If we have time, why not?"

Carly jumped in place. "Why not?"

Angie gave him a wink, pleasure filling her face. She hurried down the row, selecting a few more perennials, and after he loaded her choices in the cart, he pushed it toward the cashier.

Many times, things he longed to know flew into his head, but those kinds of questions needed time. Instead he treaded lightly. A lifetime didn't happen in a day. Angie clung to a private past she seemed unwilling to share. He could learn a lesson from her silence.

Already he'd revealed too much.

Gail Gaymer Martin is a multi-award-winning novelist, writer of contemporary Christian fiction with fifty-five published novels and four million books sold. CBS News listed her among the four best writers in the Detroit area. Gail is a cofounder of American Christian Fiction Writers, is a keynote speaker at women's events and presents workshops at writers' conferences. She lives in Michigan. Visit her at gailgaymermartin.com. Write to her online or at PO Box 760063, Lathrup Village, MI, 48076.

Visit the Author Profile page at Harlequin.com for more titles.

A Mother to Love

Gail Gaymer Martin

Recycling programs
for this product may
not exist in your area.

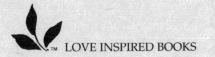

™ LOVE INSPIRED BOOKS

ISBN-13: 978-0-373-87962-5

A Mother to Love

www.Harlequin.com

Printed in U.S.A.

May the God of hope fill you with all joy
and peace as you trust in Him,
so that you may overflow with hope
by the power of the Holy Spirit.
—*Romans* 15:13

Acknowledgments

Thanks to my friend Brenda Evans who made
contact for me with Kimberly Springsdorf in
Owosso, Michigan, the executive director
of the Convention and Visitors Bureau.
Kimberly gave us a tour of the city and
showed us the highlights of the town as well as
parks and residential areas so I could find the
perfect street on which to set my story.
She answered a volume of questions and was
a valuable resource for my research for the
Lilac Circle Series. Thank you so much,
Kimberly. My thanks, too, to the lovely sales
staff at Owosso Books, Janet O'Shea and
Carla Bates, who spent time with us and
answered my questions. Thanks also to
numerous members of my Facebook group,
Readers of Gail Gaymer Martin's Books, for
their support, ideas and wonderful reviews.
A huge thank-you to my agent, Chip MacGregor.
And as always my deepest thanks and love
to my husband, Bob. Without his support
and patience (especially that), I wouldn't be
the writer I am today.

Chapter One

Angie tripped over another box and suppressed a groan. Moving was the pits. She rubbed her shin and noticed another nick to her already bruised and scraped body. She couldn't forget she'd still be looking at her piled-high boxes without the help of her coworker's toting and lugging.

Footsteps sounded on the stairs, and she pulled away from her newest wound and planted a pleasant look on her face. "How are you doing?"

"I think that's the last one." Rick Jameson came through the archway, a faint grin on his lips, nice lips she'd noticed recently. If they weren't such good friends, she could easily fall for him.

"You're the greatest." She opened her arms and headed toward him.

He stepped in and joined the friendly hug.

The flex of his strong arms beneath his T-shirt made her sigh just a little. She drew in a breath, bedazzled by the exotic scent of his aftershave. "What are you wearing?"

He drew back. "A T-shirt and jeans?"

His questioning look and response made her laugh. "I meant your aftershave."

His expression melted into a grin. He shrugged. "Jungle something. Why?"

"I love it. Flowers and foliage after rain." She arched her brow. "Good choice."

She didn't care what it was named. It smelled better than her cucumber melon moisturizer. She studied Rick's expression, wrapped in his scent, and winced. She knew she looked horrible, dressed in rags with only a swipe of lipstick and a comb run through her hair. "I'm grateful for your help, Rick."

"Anytime, Angie." He tweaked her cheek and tucked his hands into his pockets. "Anything else?"

She eyed the stacks of boxes along with another million things she needed to do, but she couldn't ask Rick for more help. She motioned to a stack. "I need to tackle these boxes myself. Most of it's for—"

Her leg vibrated before her cell phone's ringtone sounded. She drew it from her pocket and eyed the caller. "It's my sister. I'll call her back."

He shook his head. "Answer. I can let myself out."

She lifted a finger to stop him, wanting to enjoy his company just a little longer without using the time to work. She tapped the answer button and stepped into the kitchen. "Connie. Sorry, I'm busy. I have a man here helping me at the new house, and—"

"A man? What's he like?" her sister asked.

Angie cringed, realizing her mistake. "A friend. That's all." She rolled her eyes. One more offer to fix her up on a blind date and she would scream.

"Nothing serious?"

"Connie, no."

"Good, because I've found the perfect man. He's single, good-looking, a bit quiet, but—"

Her internal scream took flight. "But I'm not interested.

I've told you a hundred times. Two hundred times." Before her sister said another word, she darted back to the living room doorway, her gaze on Rick. "Anyway, I'm seeing someone right now." Her eyes locked with his.

"You are." The decibels ripped through her eardrum. "What's he like? Is he good-looking? You can't leave me hanging."

The thought of hanging sounded good at the moment—preferably Connie. "I have to go, sis. Talk later." She hit the end-call button before her sister resisted further.

She exhaled. As she gazed at Rick, her imagination soared. She wished they were… Impossible. They were friends. "Sorry." She looked at his inquisitive face, and her heart skipped. "Can I offer you a cup of coffee or something before you go?" She glanced over her shoulder at the boxes piled in her kitchen. "If I can locate the coffeemaker."

He chuckled, a sound she loved to hear. His smile and laugh always made her happy. She waited, hoping he would stay.

Rick eyed the boxes and grinned at her. "How many hours will it take?"

She managed a feeble smile, her mind still clinging to her sort-of lie. "I need the distraction." She beckoned him into the kitchen and headed for the boxes.

"Let me help." His voice came through the doorway before he did.

Rick's gaze followed her as she dug deep in a carton and, before she had a moment, he slipped the box from her hand while his eyes searched hers. She sensed he wanted to say something, yet couldn't, and it left her confused.

Without direction from her, Rick located the pot and the individual brewing cups and popped them into the machine and added water. "Mugs?"

She waved her hand at the boxes. "Your guess is as good as mine."

He shrugged and in a moment gave her a victorious look. "Voilà!" He held the mugs in his hand, then placed a cup on the coffeemaker and hit the brew button.

She loved seeing him appear comfortable making coffee and being domestic. "You surprise me."

"Why?" He glanced over his shoulder, then grasped the mug and brought it to her.

The scent of coffee eased her tension. "You look experienced in the kitchen."

"It's that or starve." He popped in another cup and turned back to her. "It's one of those things single men with a child have to do." He looked at her again before smiling and turning back to the coffeemaker.

His daughter hadn't entered her mind. Though he'd mentioned Carly on occasion, Angie sensed he would rather not talk about his situation for some reason. "Coffee tastes good."

He slipped onto a chair and set his drink on the table. "I hope you don't mind my saying this, but the phone call seemed to upset you." He glanced away. "Sorry. It's none of my business."

She flinched, facing the exaggeration she'd told her sister. "You're perceptive."

His brow arched, and he waited.

"To be honest…" And this time she would be. "I'm tired of my mother and sister trying to fix me up with blind dates. I want to scream when they come to me with some trumped-up idea of this wonderful single man who's a bit quiet but he is very nice. Usually the guy's main fun is birdwatching or reading. Nothing wrong with either hobby, but it doesn't make dating them sound particularly enjoyable."

Rick averted his eyes until a laugh burst from his chest.

He gave her a one-shoulder shrug. "Are you telling me you're not into the nice quiet bird-watcher type?" His words splintered through his chuckle.

Finally, Rick seemed like the man she knew at the office, and she needed the usual. She'd been thrown by the unexpected emotion that had arisen earlier. "Laugh all you want." She found the image funny, until the crux of the issue struck her. "Today, to stop her, I sort of lied."

"How does one sort of lie?" He gave her a crooked grin.

"You can't. I'm not much of a churchgoer, but I know right from wrong, and I feel awful." She pondered her comment.

"Explain. Now I'm curious."

His expression took the edge off her guilt. "I told her I was seeing someone."

"Seeing someone?" His face blanched and confused her. "Are you?"

She shook her head.

"Then it's not a sort-of lie."

"But I was seeing someone." She motioned to the doorway. "I stood right there and looked at you. Get it? I was seeing—"

"Right." He blinked before he added a disbelieving grin. "Got it...more than once actually."

She gave him a poke. "You know the old saying about web of lies, right?"

Questions still hung in his eyes.

"Now my sister wants details. What he looks like, his interests, everything. Next she'll want to meet him." Her head spun with her concoction. "I have to tell her what I did."

"But now she'll give you a little peace. No more blind dates."

A blast of air shot from her lungs. "You're right. It was

worth the exaggeration. That's what it was, right? Not a lie."

"Whatever you want to call it." He arched a brow again and took a long swig of his coffee. "I should get going." He stood. "But don't forget, Ang. If you need help, I'm willing." He gave her arm a shake. "I only have Carly on weekends. I hate the limited time with her, but that's our agreement, and I avoid tension with her mother. It doesn't help our relationship. For now I'm stuck with short visits." He tilted his head with a half grin, but she noted sadness beneath it. "Guess that gives you a look into my life."

"At least you've been married. Not me." Her comment drew her back to unwanted places. "And you have your little girl. I know you love her more than anything. It shows."

He responded with that proud-daddy nod. "You're right. I cherish her. And you saw how it was when my marriage ended."

"Three years ago. That's how long we worked together." She thought back. "Or was it more?"

"Four, I think. You came to the office when Carly was almost one. She's turned five and goes to kindergarten."

"Really?" The years had flown past since they'd first met.

Rick stepped toward the doorway and waved. "I need to be on my way, but remember what I said."

"I will." She followed him through the living room.

When she stepped onto the porch behind him, he turned and gave her a hug. "I hope the rest of your unpacking goes well." He added another squeeze, stepped down to the sidewalk and headed to his SUV in the driveway without looking back.

Her chest pressed against her lungs as she watched the SUV back out to the street. She still felt his strong arms around her. After she gave a final wave, she drew her gaze

from his car and stepped toward the door feeling as if she'd lost something precious.

Pulling her mind back to her empty reality, she noticed a woman heading toward her from across the street.

Her curiosity rose as the neighbor stepped onto the sidewalk and strode up her driveway toward her with a grin. Angie smiled back, guessing the woman wanted to be the first to meet the new neighbor.

"Hi." A container in one hand, the woman extended the other. "I'm your neighbor Rema."

She grasped the woman's hand. "Angela Bursten. It's nice to meet you." Her greeting stretched the truth again.

"Welcome to Lilac Circle." Rema released her hand and motioned toward the driveway. "Sorry I missed your husband. I look forward to meeting him."

"Husband?" Heat rose up her chest as she understood Rema's reference.

"I noticed him pulling away as I started across the street." Rema eyed her and grimaced. "I assumed he was your husband."

Angie drew back, managing a chuckle. "No. He's a co-worker who volunteered to tote some boxes for me. No husband here." The admission left an unwelcome reminder, yet Rick's smile hung in her thoughts.

A questioning look flashed across Rema's face, and Angie recalled Rick's hug on the porch. A sigh slipped from her. She didn't owe her an explanation and didn't have one. Warmth spread through her, and she recalled the wonderful sensation.

Rema gave her a sympathetic look.

"Speaking of boxes, I have them stacked all over inside, otherwise I'd…" Her discomfort grew as she sought an amiable goodbye. "But I appreciate your welcome, and—"

"I understand." Rema extended the container. "I brought you a little welcome gift. Homemade."

Angie's heart sank. Now she was on the spot. "That was very thoughtful." As she pulled the container closer, a sweet scent wrapped around her. "And it smells delicious." She glanced over her shoulder at the mess. "Rema, if you don't mind falling over boxes, you're welcome to come in." She opened the screen door, motioning the other woman inside.

Without hesitation, Rema slipped past and stood inside the doorway.

"Have a seat, Rema." She motioned to the living room.

Rema moved into the living room, and Angie placed the housewarming gift on a lamp table before also taking a seat, knowing what she should do but unable to deal with it today. Angie eyed the woman, trying to think of something to say, but Rema saved her from worry.

"Did you notice the house for sale on the corner?" Rema gestured to the head of the street. "We'll be having another new neighbor soon."

"No. Sorry, I hadn't noticed."

"A number of people have looked at the house. Spring seems a good time to sell." Rema gazed into space as if she had something on her mind, and though uneasy, Angie waited before trying to end their conversation and the visit.

As if awakening, Rema patted her lips with a napkin while curiosity grew in her eyes. "So why aren't you married?" Her brow fluttered to an arch before lowering. "Divorced? Or are you widowed?"

Startled, Angie organized her thoughts. She could have said she was never asked, but that wasn't something to share with a stranger. No matter, she still had hopes. Se-

rious hopes but… She dropped the thought and shrugged. "I never got around to it, I guess."

"I'm surprised. You're very pretty." Rema's admiring gaze shifted to the window as a scowl rose on her face. "But you've made a wise decision."

Angie waited for the punch line, but Rema's expression underlined her seriousness. Not wanting to broach the sensitive topic, she manipulated the conversation back to Owosso. "Tell me about the town. I've seen a few of the lovely old buildings almost set back in time, and I spotted the Curwood Castle. It's a historic town, I know, but what else is interesting?"

Rema's face brightened, but then Angie realized she might have opened Pandora's box when she needed to finish unpacking. She waved her words away. "I'm sorry, but why don't we save this for another time? I'm sure you have things to do, and I need to get to work." She rose and stacked the dishes. "Thanks so much for coming. And thanks for this wonderful treat. I'm sure it's as delicious as it smells."

Rema took her unsubtle hint and rose. "You're welcome. It's nice to have a new neighbor so close. The last person living here was a crotchety old man who sat outside giving everyone the evil eye. You're a welcome relief."

"Th-thank you, Rema. Hopefully we'll have another friendly neighbor in the house for sale down the street."

"I hope so." She put her hand on the doorknob. "I'm sure we'll be best friends soon enough."

Angie didn't know what to say, and when Rema stepped outside, Angie closed the door and caught her breath. She wanted to be neighborly without coffee klatches or hanging over the fence. She preferred being with her friends, people who meant something to her.

Rick's image filled her mind. Their friendship had blos-

somed without effort. If not for her lack of confidence in relationships, she might have given thought to him as more than a friend a couple of years earlier. Lately her feelings had strengthened even more since they'd been spending more time together outside work.

The images flying into her mind throughout the day had got out of hand. She'd never known a man so thoughtful and caring. Although they were friends, he treated her like someone significant in his life. He made her feel like a woman and not a commodity. Yet her hope fell flat when she thought about the corporation where they worked. The company didn't tolerate employee romances. She tried to forget the work awaiting her. She pulled back her shoulders and forced herself to head for the boxes. If nothing more, they would be a distraction. She hoped.

Rick folded the completed file and slid it into his desk drawer before turning off his computer. The clock hadn't alerted him of the time, but his stomach had. He rose and rolled his chair under the desk, his hunger guiding him to the company lunchroom. Although restaurants were nearby, he usually brought a lunch, finding it more economical.

As he entered he grinned to find Angie already seated. He'd learned that her stomach and his were often in sync. That wasn't the only way they were in sync, either. He faced that more and more. She'd grown as a friend and even more as someone he wanted to be with. So often she remained in his thoughts, and he liked thinking about her.

She gave him a wave as he headed to the refrigerator. With his lunch bag in hand, he settled beside her at the table, noting her sandwich of meat rolled in a lettuce leaf and a delicious-looking muffin that dripped with icing. The incongruity made him chuckle.

"What's funny?" She grinned at her lettuce wrap and

muffin as her eyebrow arched. "A welcome-to-Lilac-Circle gift from a neighbor. I can't let them go to waste." She tilted her head toward the refrigerator. "And if you don't think it's too hysterical, you might enjoy the one I brought you."

This time his brows lifted. "You did?"

She smirked. "You know I did."

He hurried back to the fridge and found the muffin in a lunch bag with his name on it. He was touched that she'd also thought of him.

With the treasure in hand he settled beside her and sipped from a juice box from his lunch bag. "I know. I was desperate." He held up the container. "It's Carly's, but I'll have another supply in the house before this weekend."

"You're a good dad, Rick." She took the last bite of her lettuce wrap, her focus shifting toward the muffin. "I think I'll get a coffee."

She slid back the chair and headed around the corner to the counter that held the coffee urn. As she hurried away, he admired her. He understood how she stayed trim. She lived like a rabbit, eating veggies and lettuce sandwiches. The occasional sweet treat was rare for Angie.

The odor of strong coffee surrounded him before she set it on the table and sat back down. "Smells like that stuff was left over from yesterday."

She took a careful sip, and her nose wrinkled. "The day before, I suspect."

They both grinned while she pulled the wrapper off the muffin. He bit into his sandwich, watching her take a bite of the luscious-looking treat. "That's from a neighbor?"

She nodded, taking a moment to swallow. "Rema, to be exact. It was very sweet of her on one hand, but not convenient." She lowered her head and brushed away her comment. "Anyway, the muffins are delicious." She swiped a

bit of icing from the edge. "You may have seen her as you pulled away."

He shook his head, recalling he'd seen only Angie standing on the porch, her eyes on him.

"The problem was the piles of boxes, and the house was a mess. And she was a bit odd."

"Odd? In what way?" Because Angie was so rarely judgmental, her comment surprised him.

"She was pleasant enough but seemed sort of sad. More like depressed." Angie's face sank to concern.

He wanted to cheer her. "Some people are sadder than others."

"And blunt."

His grin grew. "Sometimes you're—"

"No, I'm not." She gave him a coy look. "Maybe a bit, but not like this. She asked me why I wasn't married."

He drew back, agreeing it was a very personal question. "How did she know you weren't married?" He glanced at her finger, aware she'd never worn a ring as long as he'd known her.

An uneasy expression slipped across her face. "She thought you were my husband."

"Why would she think that?"

She gave a one-shoulder shrug. "We hugged on the porch, I guess. But from her other comment, I still wonder."

"Huh?" She'd stumped him, though he did recall her hug. He admired Angie's open affection, so different from Glenda's. She'd become cool after they'd married, and he'd never understood why.

"When I told her I wasn't married, she said I probably made a good decision." Her eyes widened. "Don't you think that's odd to tell a stranger?"

He did, but he sought an explanation. "I suppose it's not if she's divorced or in a bad marriage."

"You're right." She thought a moment. "Anyway, I didn't pursue the conversation."

"You didn't? What happened to your inquisitiveness?" His own was piqued, curious how Angie had explained she was still single. He'd asked himself the same question.

She rested her elbow on the table and leaned closer. "Don't worry. I'm sure I'll learn why. She told me we would be great friends."

They both grinned, and she let the conversation slide. He didn't like seeing Angie on edge. Her upbeat spirit had won his heart, and he'd befriended her for that reason, along with her ability to make the best of even bad situations. She found something positive in most everything. "Seeing your grin gave me an inspiring idea." An idea that was sort of one-sided, but she might like it. "Can you use any more help this weekend?"

"Hard to tell, but I know I want to do some things in the yard once I'm done emptying the boxes." Her expression shifted to what appeared to be interest. "Why? Are you volunteering?"

"With an ulterior motive." A guilty nudge hit his chest. He loved spending time with Angie, but he couldn't tell her that. "I have Carly this weekend, and you've never met her. Since you're out of the apartment now and in a house, I thought Carly might enjoy a yard to play in. I like to take her places, but I can never think of anything."

"Rick, I'd love to meet her, and if we plant some flowers, she could help."

"Are you sure? She's only five."

"Give her credit, Dad. Five-year-olds can do lots of things when you teach them."

"I suppose." He took his finger and dug into a hunk of the muffin. "This smells wonderful."

"It is, but my hands are sticky, and I need to get back to my desk." She jumped up, slipped her chair under the table and grabbed the lunch trash. As she passed him, she gave him an elbow and leaned close to his ear. "See you tomorrow, and, Rick, I'm really looking forward to meeting Carly on Saturday."

Since others were in the room he only nodded. He sensed that a couple of the guys figured he and Angie were a thing, even though the higher-ups discouraged coworker dating. If they only understood that a man and a woman could actually be friends without romance. The thought shivered down his back. Right now romance was off the list, but could he and Angie remain friends? And even more, did he want to be only a friend?

As the question struck him, reality sneaked in. Their work made it nearly impossible, but if he did get involved with a woman, Angie would be the only one who would interest him. No one could get to his heart as she seemed to do.

Get to his heart? Adrenaline shot through him with the impact of his thoughts. Speculation like that had to end. Between company policy and a friendship he valued, impractical emotions could put their relationship in jeopardy. And now he'd involved Carly.

He closed his eyes. It might be impractical and chancy, but the feelings were there. He had to back off or slow down. A weight struck his chest. Or throw caution to the wind and let things happen. He'd messed up by allowing himself to get involved outside work. There they could be friends. In the world, friendships could grow and burst into something wonderful.

Carly might be his guide. If she appeared uncomfortable with Angie, then he would have little choice. His

daughter needed security right now and, as her father, he had to listen.

As his thoughts sank deep, the weight grew heavier on his heart.

Chapter Two

The next day Angie hurried through the house, unpacking the last few boxes and making her living room come to life with lamps and decor except for the walls. She'd need help for that. She did everything she could to distract herself from the uneasy feeling that had settled in her.

"I'm being silly." Her voice escaped into the room. Definitely silly. She needed a fresh perspective, and her gaze shifted to the bright window where she saw the sun spilling onto the grass, trees and landscaping around her home. Though well tended, her yard lacked flowers, and those little changes would make the house her home.

Needing a break, she slipped her house key into her pocket and stepped outside. The warmth struck her arms and the scent of lilacs swept past her. The blossoms on the trees were abundant, and the aroma floated on the air. The street name had captured her if not the house itself. Who didn't love lilacs?

Deciding to get a closer look at her neighbors' flower beds, she bounced down the sidewalk and turned right toward the jog in the road, her body buoyed by a renewed spirit. Rick had helped her so much, and she had only a few things to do to finish making the house livable. The

neighborhood also lured her to anticipate new friendships even though Rema and her sadness hadn't made the most upbeat impression.

Rema hadn't dropped by since the day she'd appeared with the muffins, and Angie's concern had faded. Since her visit, Angie had noticed Rema's husband coming and going. He seemed to keep late hours and she wondered about his career…or whatever it was that kept him away.

Instead of her original attitude toward Rema, the thought of her as a wife with so much time alone and without children softened Angie's heart. One day she should invite Rema over or drop by her house for a visit. She'd never been inside any other houses on the street, and she'd like to see what they were like.

She exhaled and studied her surroundings. She looked toward the corner and noticed the house for sale did have a sold sign and she'd missed it. While her attention darted from one side of the street to the other, she admired the flower beds and the variety of foliage. She would add plants to her landscape soon. Looking at the displays today made her anxious to tackle the flower beds.

As she approached a yellow ranch, she noticed an elderly man on his knees digging into the soil, a flat of flowers beside him. Age didn't stop some people. She picked up her step as her shadow slipped past him.

He noticed and looked at her over his shoulder. "Hello, there."

She faltered, pleased to see his smiling face, which reminded her of her grandfather, long gone to heaven. She grinned back. "You're busy, I see."

He hoisted himself up, taking a moment as if to balance himself before stepping closer. "I had tulips and spring flowers here, but they're gone, so I'm adding a few more plants. If my wife were here, she'd have pushed me out

the door a week ago with her honey-do list." His eyes twinkled.

"My grandma had one of those lists, too."

His eyes searched hers a moment. "You love family, too."

She nodded, though aware she'd neglected hers in recent years.

"Too many young people go off and don't remember where they came from. Know what I mean? Their roots and their faith training tossed into the wind." He tilted his head. "Are you a woman of faith?"

Guilt crept into her heart. "I grew up in a Christian home, but I've been rather delinquent about acting on it."

"Hmm. I knew you had the foundation. Sometimes I can just tell." He gave her a wink. "I'm Elwood Barnes, but my friends call me El."

She extended her hand. "Angela Bursten, and my friends call me Angie."

El eyed his hand and brushed it off on his pants before he grasped hers. "Nice to meet you. I hope you're enjoying your new home. I think you'll like most of the neighbors." He chuckled as if he'd told himself a joke.

"I love the house." A grin stole to her mouth. "And I'll love it more when I get things settled. You know how it is." She shrugged. "I'm still finding places for everything and working out the kinks."

"I know about kinks." He did a little bounce from the knees. "I have a few of those myself."

Cute as could be, he made her chuckle. "I think you're doing well, Mr. Barnes, and I've had help moving in, so I can't complain."

He tilted his head toward the Durbans' house. "You meet Rema?"

She eyed him a moment, questioning why he'd asked.

She didn't suspect the sweet man to be a gossip. "Yes. She dropped by with some delicious muffins, and we had a short visit."

"Rema could use a friend or two." A twinkle lit his eyes. "I hope she made a good impression, and I suppose the muffins helped."

Grinning, she gave a nod as Rema's words echoed in her thoughts—*I'm sure we'll be best friends soon enough.* "I don't see her husband much."

His smile faded. "Trey…" He paused a moment. "He travels a lot. I think Rema's lonely."

Lonely. She'd been lonely, too, at times, but moving and Rick had filled her life with new expectations.

"Married?" El glanced at her left hand.

"No, not yet." Yet? "No" would have been good enough. She managed to control a frown. "But a good friend from work came over and toted the heavy stuff. He's a very kind man. Probably someone like you." Angie spotted a hint of pride puffing his chest.

"Thank you." He shook his head. "So this fella is just a good friend. Nothing else on his mind?"

An image sparked in her mind. Life with Rick? She found him attractive, but she'd avoided thoughts of anything more. At least, she tried to. "Right. Rick's just a friend, and that's good with me." But her true feelings and reactions confounded her.

"Good girl." He patted her arm as concern fell across his face. "Please, don't think I'm the nosy neighbor or the morals police. I just admire young people who value the Lord's expectations."

"My parents gave me strong values." Again she thought of her relationship with Cal and his friends. She'd let her values slip there, anticipating a ring on her finger. What

a mistake. "And I don't see you as being nosy. I think you care about people, and you're a man of wisdom."

"Thank you, but the Good Book's filled with wisdom. I just have a good memory."

His wit tickled her. "El, it's nice to meet you, and I know if I need a little wisdom I can come to you, especially with that good memory you mentioned."

He gave her a wink. "Love to have you, and you'll find other good people on this street."

She loved his smile. "I'll let you get back to work and finish my stroll so I can face mine again. I'm determined to get things put away so I can get outside, too."

He laughed and waved as she returned to the sidewalk and her trip around to the circle and back. Yet as she walked his comment about Rema being lonely knotted in her chest. Though she didn't want to take on a needy friend, she couldn't neglect her, either.

She headed back home on the far side of the street, admiring her new house as she approached. As it often did, Rick's image popped into her mind. But so did El and his encouragement to read the Bible, as if it was something she needed. Maybe it was. She'd been without the Lord for a while, and like Rema, she'd been lonely, too. Lilac Circle had opened doors for new friendship and now El had reminded her of another friendship, one with the Lord. Like all new friendships, it would take time.

Though she'd slept poorly, Angie looked forward to the day and Rick's visit. She bounced down the stairs with a sense of accomplishment. The linens lay in a closet in neat piles, her clothes stacked in drawers lined with scented paper, and her cosmetics and personal items had found their logical place in the bathroom drawers and cabinets.

She'd even settled on which paintings and wall decor would look best in each room.

The extra bedroom had become a guest room, though she rarely had overnight guests. It looked neat with the bed made and a couple of knickknacks in appropriate spots to add a little life to the room. The second floor was finished except for hanging the wall decor.

Rick's visit added a bit more hope. He could hang the pictures and anything else she'd selected to adorn the rooms while she made decisions about what to tackle in the yard.

She'd meant it when she'd told Rick she looked forward to meeting Carly. Rick seemed to dote on the little girl, and she'd learned enough to know that things weren't always smooth between him and his ex-spouse. Problems didn't make a good environment for their young daughter. Yet she had confidence in Rick. He would never do anything to hurt his daughter, so she suspected when trouble came he did all he could to hide it from Carly.

She poured coffee into a mug and nibbled on a buttered English muffin. Nothing else appealed to her. Egg? French toast? Pancakes? Although they sounded good, pancake recipes seemed to be for more than one person. She shook her head at her thoughtlessness. She should have invited Rick and Carly to breakfast.

To help pass time she busied herself by lining pictures along the walls where she wanted them hung, and she laid a couple of items on the bed that she thought might look nice in the bathroom—a cute wall clock set in a floral motif and a small shelf to hold a miniature vase and a pin box that had belonged to her grandmother. For her home office, she'd laid out a tapestry from her grandmother's home as well as a dry board to jot notes to herself.

She eyed the kitchen clock. Nine. She suspected they'd

be there soon, but with a little one, maybe not. Before she could question his arrival any longer, a sound from the driveway alerted her. She ran to the living room window and peeked out.

Her heart skipped a beat upon seeing his car. She spotted Rick leaning into the backseat, releasing Carly's booster-seat straps. The girl jumped out, cute and spunky, her eyes the same shape and hazel color as Rick's and bowed lips that must have been like her mother's. Rick's were full and more rugged than his daughter's bowed ones.

Without waiting for their ring, she hurried to the door and swung it open. At work, Rick wore a sport coat or a shirt and sweater, but today he had dressed in jeans and a deep gold polo shirt that highlighted the gold in his hair.

Rick looked up and gave a wave. "I hope we're not too early."

"Not at all. I've been up for a while." She hated to tell him she hadn't been able to sleep and had thought about his visit throughout the night. She pulled her gaze from Rick's and focused on the child. The girl had her daddy's hair, the same golden brown with cute bangs and the sides curved beneath her chin. "Hi, Carly. I'm so glad you came to visit."

The child gave her a shy look and glanced at Rick before her hazel eyes darted back to Angie. "Thank you."

Polite and sweet. Angie's heart gave a squeeze. She could see why Rick's life revolved around the little girl. "Come in. I was just having breakfast."

Rick's smile faded. "Oh, I'd hoped I would catch you before that." He lifted a paper bag she hadn't noticed. "I brought you a breakfast sandwich."

Her chest constricted. "Really? I couldn't decide what to eat, so I'm nibbling on an English muffin."

"Well, stop nibbling. I have a sandwich for each of us. Even Carly wanted to give it a try."

She stood back, holding open the door as they entered.

Rick headed straight for the kitchen with Carly on his heels. When she came through the doorway, he'd pulled three packages from the sack and eyed the coffee carafe. "Do you have enough?"

She nodded and pulled a mug from the cabinet. "Here you go, and, Carly, would you like milk or some orange juice?"

The child glanced at her dad, who gave a nod. "Milk, please."

Angie grinned and poured a glass of milk from the carton.

They gathered around the table, and when Rick bowed his head, Carly followed. As if a belated thought, he looked up. "Do you mind?"

"Mind? No, please." Angie folded her hands and waited.

Rick gave Carly a nod. The child eyed her before beginning the prayer. "Come, Lord Jesus, be our guest…"

The prayer leaped from the recesses of Angie's mind. How often had she heard those words spoken around the table? Her father's voice rang through her head and, fighting tears, she had to force herself to look up when Carly finished. "Thank you, Carly. I used to say that prayer when I was your age."

"You did?" The five-year-old looked at Rick with question. "Is the prayer really old?"

Angie pressed her lips together to control her chuckle. Rick struggled with the same reaction as he explained it was very, very old. "Even your great-grandmother knew that prayer, Carly."

The child seemed to ponder what he'd said as she delved

into her breakfast sandwich. After two bites her expression made it clear she enjoyed it.

Angie enjoyed hers, too, but then she remembered Rema's delicious muffins and wished she'd saved a couple. Maybe she'd have to learn to bake. Kids loved cookies, cake and muffins. Out of the corner of her eye, Angie watched the girl, hoping the child felt welcomed. "Carly, your daddy tells me you're in kindergarten."

Carly's face lit with a grin, the sandwich forgotten. "Uh-huh and do you know what?"

"No. Tell me." Angie leaned closer, enjoying the child's animation with her hands raised as if ready to applaud.

"Our teacher gives us fun homework."

"Fun homework?" She drew back, never remembering a time when she'd thought homework fun.

Rick's eyes twinkled. "I reacted the same way until she explained. The teacher has them go outside for activities. They had to find samples of leaves, wildflowers and acorns, and then she gave the children a list of things to find in their yards." He grinned. "See. That's fun homework."

"I imagine it is." She got a kick out of the child's exuberance.

Carly's eyes widened. "And guess what I found."

Angie shrugged. "A pinecone?"

"No. I found a dandelion."

"I remember dandelions." Angie pictured the yellow flowerlike weed, the bane of all the adults when, later, its puffy seeds landed in their yards. Yet her mind shot back to a day when her mom had put a dandelion beneath her chin and told her if it left a yellow stain she would find her true love. So much for dandelions.

Rick stood. "I noticed the house on the corner has a sold sign already."

"I saw it yesterday. A new neighbor will move in soon, I suppose."

His sandwich gone, Rick wiped his mouth and motioned toward the archway. "Which reminds me, where do we start?"

His eagerness tickled her. "How are you at hanging pictures and things?"

"A pro." He gave a playful grimace. "Okay, I'm not exactly a pro, but I'm not bad. I have a good eye, but I'm even better if you have a level."

A level? "Is that one of those wood things with the little bubbles?"

An odd expression came over his face, and then, as if a light had turned on, he chuckled. "I suppose a person could describe it that way. Apparently you don't have one."

"Apparently."

"I can eyeball it. It'll be fine."

She loved his eyes, a deep tan sprinkled with gold dust. They twinkled as if they were mischief looking for a place to happen. "I'm sure you can eyeball it. You have very nice eyes." She snapped her fingers. "How about a measuring tape? I have that along with a hammer and the right kind of nails for frames and things. I asked at the hardware store."

"Sure, a yard stick or tape measure works." He drew back his head with a tilt. "And you even asked at the hardware store."

"I did." She flashed a silly smile as he appeared to study her.

His look gave her goose bumps. Not the scary kind but the kind that confused her. His eyes drew her in as if he read her mind. And when his dimples flexed, then vanished, she sensed he'd told himself a joke, probably about her. His subtle sense of humor was one of his attributes she loved. But today only tension grasped her. She waited

to see what he'd say or tell her what he wanted, but he didn't say a word.

Instead he looked away without a response and slipped his hand into his pocket. After a moment, he took a deep breath. "Well?"

She rose from the table, buoyed with excitement. "If you're ready to get started, let's go. I don't want to hold you up from—"

"That's no problem." He winked at Carly. "You and I saved the whole day for Angie, didn't we?" She gave him a smile and nodded. "We have nothing else waiting, and we know you want to buy some flowers and get some planting done."

"I do." She pointed to the staircase. "So, let's get busy. I'll show you what needs to be done upstairs, and while you're doing that, Carly can help me decide on the flowers."

"I can?" Excitement flickered on her face along with the telltale dimples that validated she was Rick's daughter.

"Absolutely." She loved seeing the child's enthusiasm. "You can even help me plant some of them. How's that for an idea?"

"Daddy, I can help plant." She bounced on her toes.

"I know. Angie is a glutton for…" He rolled his eyes. "Never mind."

Carly tilted her head. "What's a glutting?"

"A really nice person, I think." Rick patted her head as his eyes shifted to Angie. "Let's see what you have upstairs."

She beckoned him to follow. Carly joined him as they traveled from room to room while she pointed to the various items needing to be hung.

"You really have a nice place here, Ang. I didn't pay attention when I was toting boxes."

Ang. No one had called her that since her dad had years
ago. It had been a special signal they were pals. He'd never
had the son he'd wanted, so she'd become his buddy. She
loved their relationship. He'd taken her fishing and some-
times had let her help him do minor car repairs or main-
tenance. She'd forgotten it all now, but it had meant the
world to her then.

Her mind snapped back and she shrugged. "Sorry. I
went on a short memory trip. I like it here, too. Thanks."

He gave her a playful wink and didn't seem concerned
about her distraction.

When she had finished pointing out the tasks, Carly
joined her downstairs without looking back, and they
headed outside. As she studied the yard, Carly did the
same.

Angie lifted a pen to the notepad she'd brought. "What
do you think? Where should we put the flowers?"

Carly skipped across the lawn and selected an empty
space in front of the lilac bushes that would experience
morning and early afternoon sun before being dimmed by
the shade of the foliage in late afternoon. "That's a good
spot, Carly." Her mind sought the kinds of flowers that
could work, ones that thrived with partial shade.

"Back there." Carly pointed to an area along the fence
just beyond another cluster of large lilac shrubs.

She studied the place, which would have full sun most
of the day. "That's a good place. We could plant roses."
She made a note.

Carly spun around and headed back to her. "Roses are
pretty."

"They are." She tucked her arm around the child's shoul-
ders, not sure how she would respond, but Carly drew
closer without hesitation. Angie loved the feeling of Carly
beside her and enjoyed showing affection to the little girl.

From what she'd learned from Rick, Carly's mother worked a job that resulted in travel and long office hours. The girl spent hours in an after-school program and often child-care services.

Angie's chest tightened, picturing the bubbly child, eager to please and anxious to help, being raised by people other than her mom. Angie understood that some jobs were demanding and the woman had to make a living, but she couldn't alter the emotion she felt for Carly. A lump formed in her throat and startled her. She'd been well loved by both parents as a child, and she wanted that for Carly.

She and Carly moved to the side of the house and into the front yard, where beds had once held flowers. They made notes of the kinds of plants she could buy. Though she had enough ideas to cost a fortune, she knew she could start small and add perennials each year.

Taking a break, they sat on the porch steps and talked about different kinds of flowers. Though Carly knew more about flower colors than kinds, she mentioned roses and tulips. Planting bulbs in autumn would add colorful spring blossoms to the landscape. Angie made a note in her book to help her remember.

"What do you like to do for fun, Carly?" The question came out of nowhere.

Carly looked thoughtful as if she had too many to list. Yet no ideas seemed to come.

"How about swings and slides at the park?" Angie watched her face brighten.

"We have swings at school."

"Can you go up high on them?" She watched the girl's face twist in thought.

"I don't know how." She faced Angie. "Do you?"

Tender feelings slid through Angie. "You'll learn when

you're bigger, but one day we'll have to take you to a park. Your daddy can push you a little bit high."

"Really?" Her eyes sparkled. "And can we go on the slides?"

"You can. I think I'm too big." She pictured herself trying to squeeze her hips down a slide. The picture made her smile. "Does your daddy take you to the park?"

"No, but we go shopping and buy groceries. And he takes me to the hamburger place that has tunnels and ladders, and he watches me play."

"That's fun. I don't think they had that kind of play area when I was a little girl. You're lucky."

"I am, because my daddy is fun." Her head lowered as if in thought and then popped up. "Daddy reads me stories, and we laugh. And he buys us pizza."

"You are a very lucky girl."

"Maybe he'll buy you pizza, too." She looked thoughtful before nodding her head. "I'll tell him to."

Angie silenced her gasp. "You don't have to. Let's see if he thinks of it by himself." All she needed was to have him think she'd put the bug in Carly's ear to invite her for pizza.

Carly nodded. "Okay. Let's see."

"See what?" Rick came around the corner of the house, a bright smile on his face.

"Nothing." Angie jumped up. "We were talking about playing on swings and slides at a park. Carly would like that."

His eyes widened. "Good. We have a park somewhere near us. Good idea."

She suspected Rick hadn't thought of the park. The child needed fun and ways to play, and she wondered what they did together other than grocery shop and eat burgers and pizza. Little kids needed stimuli.

His unexpected appearance surprised her. "Are you done with everything?"

"I think so. Do you want to check?"

The thought ran through her head and out again. "No. Later. Let's go to the nursery for the flowers."

"Let's go." Carly clapped her hands and skipped toward the car.

Rick reached for her, but before he captured Carly she spun away from him toward the car, wearing a silly grin as she beckoned to him to follow. A tender feeling oozed through Angie as she viewed the father-daughter antics. Though she had lost confidence in men and had no desire to marry, today a sweet sensation ran through her, and for once she understood the joy of being a family. With the image in her mind, she melted.

Rick pulled into Sunburst Garden and parked. He hadn't felt this alive in years. Carly's smile and excitement sent guilt creeping up his back. Why hadn't he thought to teach her things like planting a flower or doing simple tasks? She'd cozied up to Angie as if she was a female Pied Piper. Though logic said he should feel a bit envious, he didn't. Seeing his daughter's spirit higher than the treetops—and over such simple things—lifted him into the clouds.

He jumped from the car and headed for Carly to unhook her booster seat, but she'd already loosened the belts and slipped out of the shoulder strap as Angie opened the door for her. She bounded from the SUV, skipping around them as if she had swallowed jumping beans. The sight made him laugh. "You are a bundle of energy."

"I'm excited 'cause Angie said I can help plant flowers." Carly gazed at Angie with admiration. "I've never planted flowers."

"Okay, but if you're good at it, then I'll put you to work at home." He gave Carly a wink.

Carly loved the idea and skittered ahead of them through the nursery gate into the outdoor area filled with all types of perennial plants.

He held back, longing for time to talk with Angie, but he suspected that wouldn't be easy with Carly's exuberance.

Angie found a shopping cart and placed an empty flower flat in it and then pushed it along with Carly hanging on to the handle. Rick followed, amazed at his little girl's attraction to Angie and the whole idea of planting flowers.

Angie beckoned her toward the annuals inside the building and pointed to a flat. "See these flowers, Carly?"

She nodded. "They're pretty."

"They're called wave petunias, and they're beautiful when they grow in a garden, so I want you to pick out the colors that you like and put them in this box." Angie picked up a box of pink petunias and set them in one of the little compartments. "We'll fill this flat with all kinds of colors that you like, and they will grow so big you'll be surprised."

"I get to pick them myself?"

Angie nodded. "I trust you'll do a good job, and I'll be right here."

Rick's head spun hearing the dialogue between the two. Carly moved up and down the lengthy row, studying the plants as if she'd been asked to make a necklace from the crown jewels.

Angie stood back, an amazing smile on her face, her rounded cheeks rosy. Even without lipstick, her lips were pink. They curved in a warm smile. "Look at her, Rick. She's a little treasure."

He agreed. "I wish her mom could see this. Glenda's work keeps her busy, and sometimes I feel she pays little attention to Carly. I hope she doesn't notice." He lowered

his head and faced his own weakness. "And sometimes I don't think I'm much better."

"Come on, Rick. You're a loving person, and you dote on her when you talk about her."

"I know. I love her more than I can say, but sometimes I'm at a loss. I never would have thought to let her select flowers for a garden or help plant them. It's something a mother thinks about, I guess. Watching you, I feel inadequate."

"Stop thinking like that. You're creative. At Carly's age, she's learning all the time, and you can help teach her things she'll remember always."

"You're giving me more credit than I deserve, but thanks. I hope you're right." He touched her arm, feeling her soft skin beneath his fingers. "I'm definitely learning from you."

She gave a head shake and shifted her gaze to Carly, who'd begun to fill the flat with thoughtful choices.

"Angie." He drew in a breath, not wanting to ruin the moment or the day. "You'd make a wonderful mother. I really can't understand why some man hasn't snapped you up before now." The only thing that made him know she'd heard him was the expression on her face.

Her brow furrowed a moment before softening. "To be honest, Rick, I was never asked."

He drew back, unable to grasp what she'd said. "You're kidding. That can't be."

"But it is. I don't tell people this. Once I thought I'd found my true love, but…" She shook her head. "It wasn't meant to be, and after I looked back on it, I realized it would have been a mistake. I've never been open enough to arouse a man's interest, since…since—"

"It was the motorcycle guy, wasn't it?" He recalled the impact the man's death had on her.

She nodded. "We were too different. He knew better

than I did. I still thought he'd ask me, but he was killed before he might have." She gave him a feeble grin. "But the 'might have' is unlikely. He loved his bike, camping and hanging out with the guys and their girls. That wasn't me."

"Then what was the attraction?" The image bogged in his mind. The picture she painted wasn't the Angie he knew.

"I think it was the unknown, the surprise and unfamiliar. I was pretty straightforward. Raised to get an education and a good job. Do all the right things. Go to church. He lived on the edge, and I wished I could be more like that, but…"

"But it doesn't suit you." Angie had become a woman he admired, one who would be a wonderful mother and a loving wife, a wife who would pitch in and work toward their mutual dreams.

Dreams. The word stopped him. His dream, not hers, and he'd already warned himself. His heart sank.

"It didn't suit me. Not at all. When I really thought about the lifestyle, it frightened me. Still, I wanted to do something to stimulate my very mundane life."

"And your faith? Are you still a churchgoer?"

She looked away, tension tightening her jaw. "No, I drifted. Too far, I'm afraid."

He slipped his arm around her shoulders. "It's never too far or too late, Angie. God's bigger than that. Your faith is still there. You just put it to sleep for a while, but with sleep comes renewed energy. Faith doesn't stray too far."

Angie nodded, her gaze shifting to Carly. "You've done a wonderful job with her, Rick." She strode to Carly's side and helped her set the flat of flowers on the bottom shelf of the cart. "Now, let's look for some roses."

Carly's eyes widened. "Roses smell pretty, but they have thorns."

Rick slipped behind Carly, his hands resting on her shoulders. "Sometimes beautiful things have thorns that scare you away, but if you're really careful, they're worth all the trouble." His gaze slipped to Angie, and he sensed she'd caught the analogy. From her expression he'd surprised her as much as his admission surprised him. He caught the handle of the basket. "Which way?"

Angie pointed toward the outside, and when she turned, he followed her. They made their way down the rows and found the roses in an area close to the back of the nursery where many kinds and colors were on display. She and Carly studied the plants, and Angie settled on some Knock Out roses, which she said bloomed all summer. Carly picked out some long-stemmed blossoms.

"Good choice, Carly," he said. Angie signaled him to lift the plants into the cart while she watched Carly study other ones. An expression on her face warned him she had something on her mind. "Are you sure you want all these?"

"I love them." She smiled at Carly. "This young lady did a good job of choosing some beautiful roses. But..."

When she faltered, he knew he'd been right. "But what?"

Angie eyed Carly before answering. "It'll take a long time to plant these, and I'm thinking that today may not be the best day."

He raised an eyebrow, letting her know he suspected she had left some things unspoken. "How long can flowers sit without being planted?"

"No more than a day or so. I'll need to keep them watered."

"What about tomorrow? Carly and I could come after church and finish the job." His pulse skipped at his impulsiveness. She may have had enough of them. "That's if you'd like us to."

Her face brightened. "I'd love you to come if you really don't mind."

Carly's eyes sparkled. "Can I help?"

"You sure can." Angie slipped her arm around Carly's shoulders and gave her a hug. "I've never had such a good helper in my whole life."

"Daddy." Carly bounced on her toes. "Can we come tomorrow?"

"If Angie wants to put up with us another day, we sure can."

Carly clapped and twirled, then grabbed the handle of the cart and eyed Angie. "Are we done?"

"If you're planting tomorrow, I have a few more ideas." Angie chucked Carly under the chin. "What do you think?"

Carly gave a nod and waited for her to point the way.

They followed Angie down another row while his own excitement grew. With Angie's willingness for them to return Sunday, he wanted to twirl down the rows as Carly had done. Two days with Angie felt like a gift to him as well as Carly. She made life fun and meaningful. Yet a flicker of concern tightened in his chest. He had to be careful. He'd already feared her hesitation to plant today was because of something he'd said.

"If we're finishing the planting tomorrow..." She paused and looked at Carly. "We might have time to go to the park today."

"The park? Really?" A gleeful giggle escaped Carly. "Can we, Daddy?"

"If we have time, why not?"

Carly jumped in place. "Why not?"

Angie gave him a wink, pleasure filling her face. She hurried down the row, selected a few more perennials, and after he loaded her choices in the cart, he pushed it toward the cashier. Many times things he longed to know

flew into his head, but those kinds of questions needed time. Instead he trod lightly. A lifetime didn't happen in a day. Angie clung to a private past she seemed unwilling to share. He could learn a lesson from her silence. Already he'd revealed too much.

Chapter Three

When the doorbell rang Angie hurried from the bedroom and raced down the stairs. Rick must have forgotten something, although she hadn't noticed anything. Her mind had been on their wonderful day together and how cheery and alive her yard looked.

She swung open the front door, a smile on her lips, but her jaw dropped. "Rema."

"Did I frighten you?" Rema stared at her, her hand on the screen door handle.

"No, not really." She regained her senses and pushed open the door. "I wasn't expecting anyone. I'm a mess." She gestured to her dusty jeans and soiled knit top. "I've spent the day toting flower flats and plants. I was about to take a shower."

Rema took a step deeper into the house. "I dropped by to give you some brochures about Owosso. Remember? You'd asked and I happened to be near the chamber of commerce, so I stopped."

Angie grasped the stack of colorful leaflets, pleased Rema had remembered. "Thanks so much."

"Happy to do it, and I also wanted to tell you how excited I was to see you bringing home all the new plants.

They will really make a difference. The previous owner didn't do much. I think last year he planted marigolds. Yellow ones. They remind me of dandelions."

Angie chuckled, recalling her conversation with Carly. "They do resemble them a little, but some of the outside critters stay away from them. They don't like the smell."

"The critters have better taste than the grouchy neighbor. Now I look forward to seeing lovely flower beds." Rema grinned, which looked strange on her since her brow was often furrowed with sadness. She took another step toward the living room as if she planned to stay.

Recalling the elderly neighbor's comment about Rema, Angie didn't have the heart to turn her out despite her need to shower and change her clothes. "Would you like to come in for a couple of minutes? As you can see, I really need a makeover."

Rema didn't respond. As if missing the hint, she took another step deeper inside, her eyes aimed at the living room.

"Let's go to the kitchen. I hate to sit in there covered with dirt. Anyway, it's closer to the coffeepot. Or would you prefer a glass of lemonade."

"Lemonade sounds nice."

Rema followed her into the kitchen and settled on one of the chairs. "I saw that man again. Your coworker."

She nodded, not wanting to get into her relationship with Rick. She kept her back to Rema as she pulled glasses from the cabinet and lifted the lemonade pitcher from the refrigerator. When she filled the glasses, she carried them to the table and joined Rema.

"This time he had a little girl with him."

"Carly. She's five."

A faint frown eased to her face. "Is he married?"

The question had a curious tone, not judgmental as much as troubled.

"He's divorced. It was his wife's decision, I believe."

"Divorced." She pressed her lips together. "I see." She looked thoughtful for a moment. "It's difficult when children are involved." She glanced away. "It makes me happy I don't have children even though I'd always wanted them."

Angie gathered the puzzle pieces, hoping to decipher the message wrapped up in her comments. "But you're not divorced, Rema, are you? I thought—"

"No." She shook her head back and forth as if she forgot how to stop. "No, but I feel as if I am sometimes."

Another puzzle piece. "I don't understand."

"My husband travels for the company, and he has late business meetings when he's home. I spend much of my time…" She gave her head one more shake and stopped. "Sorry. You don't want to hear my sad story."

The comment made her think of Rick's wife, who traveled for her career. "I have no advice, Rema, but I can listen." As the words left her mouth, she wished she'd not spoken. But she'd said exactly what a caring person should say. Rick would have listened for hours. She wished she were more like him.

"I think sometimes I scare people away with my negative attitude." Moisture formed in Rema's eyes. "I have to learn to make the best of things and not be so suspicious."

Suspicious. Angie could only guess what that meant, and she steered away from the topic. "Sometimes we spend our time with things that give us pleasure and then feel guilty." Words flapped from her mouth without thought. She knew so little about being alone, because it didn't usually bother her. She'd found comfort in the quiet. But had she really enjoyed being alone or only found it an easy an-

swer to her singleness? "Do you have hobbies or activities that you enjoy?"

"No. Trey likes me home…" She faltered. "But a hobby is a good idea."

Trey wanted her home. Why? The obvious answer made her sick—that he wanted to control his wife a little too much. "Community colleges provide classes for lifelong learning. Libraries offer fun classes—journaling and scrap-booking. Yarn shops teach knitting, and stained-glass stores often have classes. You can even learn to tap-dance."

Rema chuckled. "I'll have to give it some thought. Classes could fill up a lonely evening."

Her heart in her throat, Angie managed a pleasant grin. "You can even learn a job skill. Have you ever thought of—" Her cell phone's ringtone sounded, and she glanced at the ID. "It's my mom, Rema. I should answer."

"Take it and thanks for the ideas." Rema rose and gave a wave as Angie hit the answer button. "Hi, Mom. My neighbor is just leav—"

"Connie said she called about a nice fellow she knows, but you said you're dating someone. Why haven't you told us about this? You know I want—"

"Mom, you want more grandkids, I know." Angie rose and headed toward the front door to wave goodbye to Rema. "But please let me fall in love first."

"Who is he? What's his name?"

She saw Rema already across the street and heaved a sigh. "I'm not in love. I said I'd like to fall in love before having children." Though no one was there to see her, she rolled her eyes.

"Remember, Angie, you're thirty-three. Child bearing is—"

"Mom." She tripped over her exasperation. "Let's start with falling in love and getting married first. Okay?"

"But Connie said you're dating someone."

The lie bit her again. "I told her I was seeing someone. I didn't say 'dating.'"

"What's the difference?"

Angie closed her eyes and drew in a lengthy breath. "Could we talk about this another time? I was at the nursery all day with Rick…for flowers for my garden, and—"

"Rick." The sound of triumph flew through the phone. "So that's his name. When can we meet him?"

"Not today. He's gone, and I'm dirty from toting flower flats. How about if I talk with you tomor…another time. I can tell you more then."

A puff of air traveled through the phone. "Finally, you're willing to tell us about him. Okay, but don't wait too long. Remember your age and—"

"Another time, Mom. I really have to take a shower. Love you."

"Love you, sweetheart."

She hit the end-call button before her mother could ask another question. Ignoring her dirty jeans, she plopped onto the sofa and eyed the carpet. She hated treating her mother that way, but Connie and their mom wouldn't take no for an answer. Her mother still thought of her girls as teenagers, coming home after a date and facing a grilling session even though Connie was now a mom. Not that her mother didn't trust them. She enjoyed hearing of their dates and made the reveries hers.

Angie pressed her back against the cushion, her mind knotted in her mother's curiosity and Rema's marriage struggle. She couldn't help but think of the sweet elderly neighbor down the street, filled with more wisdom than anyone. His name had slipped her mind, but his comment had stuck with her—many neighbors were nice. That was

what he'd said, and she was certain he would put Rema on that list.

She smacked the side of her head. Elwood. That was his name. He'd said to call him El, and she would since she needed a wise friend on Lilac Circle. Maybe she could steer Rema down the block to talk with him. Everyone needed a special friend, a confidant, and especially a wise one.

She had Rick. She always felt wonderful when he was around, whether at work or even home. It had happened on his first visit when he'd helped her move. Rick had become a gift, a great friend she hoped to have always. She trusted him more than she'd trusted any man. Really trusted him. She loved the warm feeling that spread through her when he was near. Tomorrow she'd see him again, and she would tell him about her crazy family who wouldn't listen. Maybe he would have the wisdom to offer her a solution.

Rick eyed the blinking voice-mail notification light on his home phone and frowned. He rarely had calls on the line and often thought he should have it disconnected. He hit the first message and was struck by his ex-wife's irate voice. "This is Glenda. Please call me now."

His back stiffened with her command. The next message followed.

"Where are you? I need to talk with you. It's important."

It's important. His stomach knotted at the concern in her voice, and he glanced behind him to make sure Carly was preoccupied brushing her teeth and getting ready for bed.

Another message plowed through the line. "Richard. If you're upset with me for some reason, can you forget it and call me? Stop being silly and playing games. Call me now."

He bristled, angry at himself for allowing her to tear him to shreds. She had his cell phone number, but she never used it. A fourth message began and when he heard her

voice he covered the receiver until the call ended and de-leted all of them, irritated that she'd accused him of being angry and playing games. He rarely got angry at anyone but himself. Why would she think he was playing games? She knew him well enough to know he wasn't a game player. Far from it.

Rather than drag out the situation with more of her calls, he hit her number on his cell and listened to it ring. After the fourth ring, he expected it to go to voice mail. Not wanting to leave a message, he pulled the phone from his ear and moved his finger to the end-call button, but Glenda's voice stopped him. "I've called and called, Rick. Why are you ignoring me?"

He pressed the phone to his ear. "What are you talking about, Glenda? I have a cell phone, and you know to call me on it. I've asked you more than once. I wasn't home, so how would I know I have calls?"

"Where were you? Dragging my daughter around to—"

"Our daughter." He cringed at the accusation. "Glenda, Carly belongs to both of us. We both love her beyond words." He swallowed the burning bile in his throat. Again he glanced toward the doorway to make sure he was alone. "I was out, but you can be sure Carly is in good hands. In fact, she had a wonderful time. Would you like to talk with her and ask?"

"No. It's too late now."

His fingers ached from gripping the phone. He could do without the bitterness that continued to grow in their relationship. "What was important?"

"I had a wonderful event I wanted to share with Carly tonight, but you messed it up. It's too late now, obviously. You could have returned my call."

He shook his head. He knew better than to try to reason with her. She was unwilling to give an inch, not even to common sense. "Maybe you should plan these wonderful

events when she's with you. You know I have her some of the weekend."

He clamped his teeth around the comments he longed to say. Having Carly every weekend would be perfect. Having her every day would be better. The old discussion seemed unending, and he could attract more bees with a spoonful of sugar than a cupful of vinegar.

"Glenda, let's not argue over something that apparently is too late to fix." He drew in a deep breath. "First, this is my time with Carly, which is very limited in comparison to your many days with her. I haven't fought you on that, as you know, even though I would like to have her with me more. So when things happen ahead of time, we could trade weekends or add another weekend to her visit with me, but you can't expect me to drop my plans at the last minute. Let's be adult about this and—"

"I'm trying to be adult about this, Richard, but you don't return my calls and, as you said, it's pointless."

His shoulders slumped with his useless attempt to resolve the problem. "You're right. Whatever you say. It's late, and I'll say good-night. You'll have Carly back after school on Monday. I'll drop her clothes by the house on the way to the school. Sleep well." Without waiting for an argument, he clicked the end-call button and dropped into a chair.

"Was that Mom?"

Carly's voice shattered his attempt to hide the newest fiasco. He gave her a fleeting look and a faint nod.

"She's upset again." She sailed across the floor and climbed onto his lap. "I'm sorry, Daddy."

His heart melted. "Please don't be sorry, sweetie. It's not your fault. If Mom wants something, she knows to call my cell phone, but she forgets and—"

"She doesn't forget." Her head swung back and forth like a swinging door. "Mom does what she wants."

He drew her into his arms and held her close without a word. A five-year-old had more wisdom than her parents at times. The situation broke his heart, and a stab of regret nailed him to the chair. Something had to be done, yet he felt helpless. How could he show Glenda that they needed better communication? Their arguments didn't give Carly a sense of well-being. "I love you, sweetheart."

"I know you do." She leaned up and kissed his cheek. "I love you, too." With her head on his shoulder, she sat without speaking while his mind twisted and turned with longing and a prayer that the Lord could find an answer that wouldn't drag Carly into court as a witness in a case that pit one parent against the other. Glenda knew him too well. She'd love him to be out of the picture entirely. She seemed to do anything she could that might cause him to back away and give up, because she knew he didn't want to put their dear daughter through the mess. He could never hurt Carly that way.

"Daddy?"

"What, angel?" Wisps of her soft burnished hair brushed his neck.

"I had fun today. I like Angie 'cause she let me pick out the flowers for her garden, and when we got back she asked if we could go to the park, and you said yes. I loved the slide." She put her hand over her mouth and chuckled. "Angie tried to do it, too, but she was too big for that little slide."

Though he chuckled with her, his chest constricted. "She is a nice lady."

Her head tilted upward, her grin marred by a growing frown. "Daddy?"

"What, my girl?" He feared she would say what he suspected had been on her mind, but hoped he was wrong.

"Why can't Mom be like Angie? Mom doesn't show

me how to do anything, and if she wants me to do something, she hollers at me 'cause she's too busy to teach me."

A vise bound his lungs. "Some people don't have the same amount of patience as other people. I guess Angie has lots of it."

"Lots and lots." Carly's head bounced like a yo-yo. "We'll see her tomorrow, but can we visit her again other times? She's fun."

"I'm sure we can." He ruffled her hair. "Now I think it's time for one young lady that I love with all my heart to go to bed."

Her frown vanished, replaced by a grin. "That's me, isn't it?"

"You know it is. You're the only young lady I love with all my heart."

"I love you with all of my heart and fingers and toes." She leaned forward and kissed his cheek before hopping down. "Good night, Daddy."

"Good night, sweetheart. I'll be there in couple of minutes to tuck you in."

She walked backward toward the doorway. "I know. You always do." She giggled and spun around.

When she had vanished through the archway, Rick sat for a moment, catching his breath and willing his sadness to go into hiding. He hadn't cried in years, but tonight, the desire was strong. Racked with frustration, he stared at his hands, hands that were tied by attorneys, courts and judges. But he'd win somehow. He just had to find the way.

Hot coffee sputtered from Angie's mouth when the phone rang. She was careful with the first cup in the morning. It was always too hot, but the phone's ring made her jump and slosh it. She swiped a paper napkin across her mouth and went in search of her cell phone. She grabbed it on the

fourth ring. Her heart lurched when she saw Rick's number in the window. "Hi. Is something wrong?"

"Not from this end, but I think I woke you, didn't I?"

"No, I was in the kitchen with my first cup of coffee." She glanced at the clock, surprised he'd called so early. "If nothing's wrong, then what's right?"

He chuckled. "We're getting ready to leave for church in about fifteen minutes, and I realized I should have suggested this earlier. It hit me a few minutes ago. I wondered if you might like to go to church with us. Now, I know that you said—"

"Rick, that wouldn't stop me from joining you, but I slept in today. I'm not dressed and haven't had a bite to eat, so I'd better say no." She sensed his disappointment. "But ask me again, okay?"

"Sure. I knew this was a long shot. Carly really enjoyed her time with you, and I wanted you to know."

Her chest tightened as she pictured the child's gleaming face as she'd helped select the garden flowers and enjoyed their outing at the park. "She's delightful, Rick. I had fun, too. She brought back the girl in me. You saw me on the slide."

"She does good things for both of us." Though he'd given a faint chuckle, his voice faded at the end of his sentence.

She sensed something wasn't quite right. "What's up? I hear stress in your voice."

"You have good ears." He paused a moment. "I was checking to make sure Carly's out of earshot. I had four, maybe five, calls from her mother last night. She left voice mails on my landline. It threw me. I was so frustrated I couldn't sleep."

He filled in the details, and her pulse skipped over the tension he'd dealt with not only last night but other times during his marriage. None of it was her business, and

though she wanted to make things better for him, running down his former wife and Carly's mother wouldn't be kind or appropriate. "I'm so sorry, Rick. I know that you want the best for Carly, and I suppose her mother wants the same, but her way. Maybe someday you'll get lucky... blessed to have a solution to undo the situation. Carly belongs with you."

"I pray, Angie."

She heard him breathe, but he didn't speak. She waited, a helpless feeling growing in her chest.

"I'd better go. We need to leave for church. Thanks for listening. I'm sorry to dump all this on you. Maybe you made a mistake being a good friend to—"

"Hold on, Rick. Like the cliché says, what are friends for? You listened to me and volunteered to come to my aid with many things. You've gone above and beyond the call of a coworker, don't you think?"

"But that's different. I enjoy your company, so it's not a hardship for me."

It wasn't a hardship for her, either. She'd never enjoyed a man's company as much, not even Cal and his motorcycle pals. "Enjoying your company is mutual, especially since I adore your daughter."

Silence.

Why had she been so direct? "Rick, I appreciate your kindness, too."

"I know. You just touched me with your comment about Carly. It's wonderful to hear someone say they adore her."

"I'm hooked. You know the old hook, line and sinker? That's me."

He chuckled. "To be honest, Carly had tons of fun. So if you have things we can do other weekends, let us know."

"I can always find work but even more, I would love fun days with Carly."

"I'd like that, too."

His voice had a zing to it that she hadn't heard lately. "So would I."

"We'll see you after church if you still want us."

"Want you? I'm counting on it." Her heart smiled despite her sorrow for his situation.

When they ended the call, she sank into the chair, eyed her coffee that was now cool enough to drink, but her stomach had knotted. Confused, she leaned back and searched her head for meaning. She had planned to stay uninvolved with men until she had a grip on her life and knew what she wanted from it. She'd failed already, and it troubled her. She had to keep a grip on her involvement, and even more, her emotions.

She sipped the lukewarm coffee while her mind reeled. Rick had become a good friend, and though that was what he was now, she'd taken a big step by allowing his daughter to become involved in her life. She'd never planned to be involved with a child, and even if she married, she had always questioned being a mother. In the long haul, being a mother meant devotion and unbending love. She'd always loved her independence, and a mother didn't have independence. She had responsibility and dependents.

Yet, for the first time in her life, she wished she was a mother. She'd loved her time with Carly, yet she doubted it would last. But now she faced the truth. A child could bind a heart into a bundle and tie it with a big pink ribbon. Tearing the ribbon off would hurt the child as much as tearing herself apart. She needed to learn how to be a friend without commitment.

A friend without commitment. The idea seemed practical, very logical, but she feared impossible. Some people she knew were only on a skin level. They could be brushed off or washed away. But others were like an addiction.

They could sink inside, enter the veins and become part of the heart. Tearing them away would be worse than a hurt. It could destroy. So what should she do now? Was it too late? Did she still have a choice?

Rick held Carly's hand as they walked from the church. Although he'd heard much of the lessons and sermon, his mind often had slipped into the past days with Angie. How many times had he cautioned himself not to get involved? He had too much on his plate dealing with Glenda's moods, and though he understood them at times, he'd lost his patience.

When Carly was hurt by their relationship, his anger jarred his conscience. A child of five shouldn't carry the burden of her parents' relationship, yet she was. Carly was too wise for her years.

His thoughts shifted to his daughter bouncing beside him. Her energy had been suppressed during the worship service, and for a kid, that was like handcuffs. She was a wonderful child and had entertained herself with one of the bags the church kept in the entry to entertain younger children.

During the service, he'd spotted Carly looking at him out of the corner of his eye, a grin on her face. She'd pointed to a picture in a storybook, and he'd grinned back when he saw a drawing of Jesus surrounded by little children. Carly touched the picture of a young girl with blond hair and then had pointed to herself. His pulse had lurched and he'd nodded, then had forced himself to focus on the pastor's lesson for the day.

Nothing in the world meant more to him than the time he spent with Carly. His chest tightened, picturing Angie and how much he enjoyed being with her. Spending time with both of them had been perfect, and Angie made it so

easy. She'd admitted she loved Carly. What more could any father hear than that?

"Are we going to Angie's now?"

Carly's voice sank into his mind. "We are. She's waiting for us to do what we promised."

"Plant flowers, and I get to help."

"She couldn't do it without you, could she?" He grinned at her glowing face.

"No, 'cause I follow directions and work hard."

He nodded, his mind slipping away again to Glenda and their situation. She was missing too much with Carly, he feared. Her work and long hours kept her away and... He pushed the thought out of his mind. It was a new day, and he wanted to focus on that.

"Daddy."

"What, sweetie?" Irritated with his distraction, he paused and looked at her.

"Maybe we'll do more than planting." Her eyes filled with question.

"Maybe. Angie often has surprises for us, doesn't she?"

She nodded. "I wish Mom had surprises. But she's tired a lot, and she likes me to be quiet." She kicked at a pebble in the church parking lot. "I'm not noisy."

A chuckle escaped before he could stop it. He managed a serious look. "You're not noisy. You just have fun. That's what kids should do, and you ask lots of questions." They'd reached the car and he hit the remote.

She grabbed the door handle and grinned. "Asking questions makes me smart."

He chuckled again but this time didn't stop it, and she giggled too as she climbed into her safety seat.

Angie stood a moment watching Carly mimic her as she dug the hole and placed a plant in it, then replaced the

dirt and patted it down. The child caught on fast. "You're doing a very good job, Carly. You amaze me."

"Really?" Her expression rang with anticipation as she held the trowel over the mound of dirt she'd just removed.

"Really. You're a good learner."

Her gaze shot toward Rick. "Daddy, I'm a good learner."

She flashed him a smile that rent Angie's heart. The child loved approval and validation that she was smart and beautiful.

Rick beamed. "You are, and I'm very proud of you." He lowered his head a moment. "I think I should spend more time showing you how to do things." He knelt beside her. "What do you say?"

"I say yes." Her eyes widened. "I want to learn to bake cookies." She dragged her tongue over her lips. "Can I learn that, Angie?"

"You sure can. Maybe we could have a lesson. Would that be fun?"

Carly's eyes twinkled, and with a happy nod she set a flower in the hole, pushed the earth back and patted it before she dug another one.

Angie shifted out of Rick's way as he rose. His expression appeared a conflicting blend of pleasure embedded in sadness.

"I've done a disservice to her, Ang."

The nickname tickled her again. "No, you haven't. She wasn't ready to learn much until now. She's in kindergarten, and it's the beginning of learning for her." Angie's heart grew heavy observing Rick blaming himself. His handsome face twisted with guilt, and she wanted to take him in her arms to soothe away his concerns. "Don't be down on yourself. Instead you can start giving her opportunities to learn, but don't be disappointed if she isn't ready to grasp everything."

He shook his head, his eyes searching hers. "How do you know so much about kids? You seem a natural."

"Natural? Not really." Again his negativity about himself encouraged her to soften her explanation and to bolster him. Rick had much to offer anyone. His gentle nature and patience with everyone but himself made her ache for him. "My sister has kids. But it's instinctual, I guess." She really didn't know, but it all seemed logical. Rick calling her a natural seeped into her mind and butted against her own doubts about being a good mother. Maybe she should listen. She hoped he would do the same.

Dropping the thought, she motioned toward Carly. "While she's still working there, let me show you where I'd like the rosebushes." She beckoned Rick to follow to the back fence. She pointed to the sunny area Carly had suggested the day before and found a couple of slender twigs that she inserted into the soft soil along the fence. "This gets good sun all day, and that's what roses need, so let's plant them here. You'll need a fairly large hole so the roots can spread." She showed him a few things she knew about planting roses, techniques she'd learned from her dad.

When she checked Carly's progress, she bent down and told her they were heading around to the front, where she would mark a few more places roses would grow.

Carly seemed to love being trusted to work alone for a few minutes, and Rick joined Angie as she headed for the front.

Rick kept his focus on the driveway as they walked. "Sorry, I seem to be a downer lately." He continued to avert his gaze.

"You're not a downer. Everyone needs someone to talk with. You know my life isn't perfect."

He chuckled. "But you handle it better. Anything new going on with you?"

"Nothing new. It's the same old problem. My mom called yesterday after you left. Well, really after Rema left." She gave him a silly smile, trusting he'd understand. "As always, Mom repeated everything she'd heard from Connie."

"And now you're dealing with your sort-of lie, right?" The tone of Rick's voice harbored a laugh.

She hung her head, wishing she could laugh with him. "I guess. She said she heard I was dating, and why didn't I tell her?" After relating their conversation, she faced the inevitable. "But here's the kicker. I told her I'd talk to her later because I'd been out all day with Rick picking out flowers and needed a shower."

He guffawed.

Grinning, Angie jammed her fists into her waist. "So you already know what I'm going to say, don't you?"

"Who's Rick? That must be the guy." He grinned back. "Am I right?"

"You know you are." She rubbed her hand over her face. "So what do I do now? Do I create some guy named Rick or just confess?"

"I could help out if you think it would work."

She tilted her head. "How?"

"Number one, I am Rick. The real thing." He patted his chest. "I could hang out here a little and pretend I'm your new—what do you call it?—love interest." He studied her. "Unless that would make you more uncomfortable." He searched her eyes.

"Not at all, but I'd hate to trouble you, Rick. I'm a big girl and I can—"

"I know you can admit your exaggeration." He gave her a wink, forcing her to face her out-and-out lie. "But does admitting you lied help the original problem?"

"Original?" She searched his face until it dawned on her. "You mean the constant pressure to go on a blind date."

"Right." He shrugged and grinned. "But maybe that's what you should do."

Though he'd managed a smile, she didn't hear enthusiasm in his voice. He knew that wasn't what she wanted. "Or I can keep saying no, but that does get tiresome."

"I've been hanging around here anyway, and I'm sure you'd like to end—"

"No. No. I really enjoy your company. I told you that. Why would you say—"

"Hold on. That's not what I meant."

"What did you mean?"

"I meant I'm sure you'd like to end the calls from your sister and mother wanting you to go on blind dates." A sly look stole to his face.

A nervous titter sprang from her. "You're right, but I do want to emphasize it's been fun with Carly coming along. I never thought I would enjoy being with a child, because I've always been self-sufficient and… I don't know. I never felt motherly, but I'm learning some things about myself since Carly's visits. I'm enjoying her so much. My sister's kids are cute, but they've never 'cottoned to me,' as my dad would say. Plus they're really spoiled, and I have a hard time with that."

"You have a hard time with that?" Rick pressed his lips together, still unable to hide his chuckle.

"What?" She shrugged, a questioning look on her face. "Yes, I do like things my way, but does that mean I'm—" She held two fingers an inch apart. "Maybe I'm a tiny bit spoiled but not like Connie's kids."

"You just have opinions that you value. Let's call it that."

He knew her too well. "Let's." She grinned, loving his sense of humor. "I appreciate your offer very much. If it comes down to that I'll let you know." Her grin faded. "I

hate using you, Rick. You might want to find someone, and then I'll be in your way."

"You really think so?" His eyes searched hers.

The look sent prickles down her arms. "Who knows? Surprises happen."

He stepped closer and slid his arm around her shoulders. "They sure do." He gave her a squeeze and eased back.

The possible meaning behind his comment caught her off guard. Certain she was wrong, she linked her arm to his and motioned toward the backyard. "We'd better see what Carly's up to, and, anyway, I promised to teach her cookie baking."

"Tonight?"

"I think I did." She studied his expression. "Unless you have other plans?"

"Plans besides eating homemade cookies? No. Nothing as important as that."

She tapped her forehead with her finger. "And I might even come up with something more nutritious for dinner."

"What's more nutritious than homemade cookies?"

He could always make her smile. "I can't think of a thing."

They headed back to Carly, but amid the playfulness, her head was spinning with the turn in their conversation. Being more than friends could be a problem with their company watchdogs. But that might not have been what he was insinuating. Maybe her imagination had got away from her.

Chapter Four

Rick waited in the living room while Carly washed her hands and slipped into a fresh top. She'd done a good job keeping her pants clean. Outside, he'd brushed off the little bit of dirt, and she'd looked fine.

When they returned to the kitchen, Angie also had changed into new pants and a shirt the color of the lilacs now enhancing the landscape on Lilac Circle. Angie looked great in the color. "Do you know who thought of planting the whole street with lilacs?"

Angie swung around, her expression one of surprise. "I have no idea." She tilted her head as if in thought. "But I know who might know the answer. I'll ask the sweet man down the block. He seems to know the town, and it will give me another reason to visit him."

"You're not replacing me, are you?" He flinched a little over the brash statement, but then covered his reaction with a grin. "We'd miss doing all your dirty work."

Tension slipped away when she grinned back. "Never. Cheap labor is hard to come by."

Relieved, he drew in the scent of dinner. "What's that wonderful smell?"

"Hand moisturizer." She gave him a wink and motioned to the counter. "Slow cookers work miracles."

Carly skipped across the room and gazed at the pot. "How slow is it?"

Angie muzzled a laugh. "Not so slow that we can't eat pretty soon." She drew Carly into her arms. "Are you hungry?"

Carly glanced at him before she nodded.

"Good, and we'll eat faster if everyone pitches in." Angie pointed toward him. "You're our salad maker. Everything's in the fridge."

"Where are your bowls?" He eyed the numerous cabinets.

In moments Angie had pulled out a large bowl, a cutting board and knife, lowered the temperature of something on the stove and given him a poke. "Carly and I will set the table."

Carly's eyes widened. "I get to set the table."

While he started to work, his heart swelled watching Angie set out the plates and silverware and asking Carly to put them around the table. She didn't seem to care how she set it. The woman had a way with kids.

In moments he had the semblance of a salad, and Angie had filled a bowl with brown rice for something. She'd never told him what was in the slow cooker, but he would know soon enough. They gathered around the kitchen table, his pride spiking when he noted that Carly had done a great job dispersing the dishes and silverware.

"Would you like to bless the food?"

Carly said the prayer again and the meal began. The mysterious entrée had been worth the wait, chicken breasts covered in a rich creamy Mexican salsa sauce. "This tastes even better than it smells."

Carly nodded, digging her fork into a mix of rice and chicken. "This is better than pizza."

"Whoa." He widened his eyes, surprised to hear her admission. "Now, that's a compliment."

They talked about the progress in the garden, the meal and the brochures Angie's neighbor had brought over for her to learn more about the town. His heart warmed at the sight of the three of them seated together around the table as if they were a real family, each contributing to the subject matter and listening in turn.

Pleasure glowed on Carly's face. When they were alone, he often sank into thoughts about his frustration over wanting to be with Carly more and being unable to arrange it. Sometimes, Carly called to him, which helped him get out of his own head. But not today. The day made him long to be a real family again, to find someone who loved him and his daughter.

He looked at Angie, his joy sinking. She had never given him an inkling that he was any more than a good friend. A wise decision, he had to admit, since he had no idea how their company would react if their relationship changed.

For now, he would keep it light. And he would love every moment of it.

"Here are some options."

Angie's voice roused him. "That sounds dangerous."

"What's options?" Carly looked from one to the other, her curiosity evident.

Angie chuckled and patted Carly's hand. "Two things we could do and you get to pick."

"I get to pick? Sometimes I get to pick with Daddy."

"Today I'm letting you make the decision." Angie rose and got the brochure she'd left on the counter. "Here's what we can do." She opened the flyer. "We could go to Bentley Park." She eyed him. "Do you know where it is?"

He shrugged. "I think so. It's on South Shiawassee Road."

"Do you know what they have at that park, Carly?"

Her eyes widened. "Swings?" Her voice piped with excitement.

"Swings and more. Lots more. It's called a Playscape with a special place for children who are five years old."

"Me." Carly nearly tipped over her chair.

Her exuberance caused all three of them to laugh.

"Don't get too excited, Little Miss. Remember you have options. Choices."

Her grin faded, and she lifted her eyes to Angie. "What else?"

"You wanted to bake cookies and I'm not sure we'll have time for both."

She glanced at him as she spoke. "Can I bake cookies another day?"

He tilted his head toward Angie. "You'd better ask our hostess."

"Can I?"

Carly's pleading expression made Angie bite her lip. "Certainly. I'd love that."

Carly slipped from the chair and twirled around. "I pick the play place."

"Playscape it is." Angie rose and he followed, rinsing dishes and putting away the food before they left.

His spirit soared as high as Carly's but he managed not to twirl around as she had. Their lives had changed, and though his heart may have tangled in dreams, a special friendship meant just as much to him for now. He had to hold on to the complicated longing, but a dream was worth fighting for. He hoped the Lord had the same idea in mind.

Rick gaped at the Playscape, as did she and Carly. Angie had studied the brochure and the photo, but seeing the

amazing children's play area inspired her as she thought of the cost, work and love the community had shown for the children.

Carly unlatched her seat belt before Rick turned off the engine. "Can I climb up the tower?" She grasped the door handle and bounded out almost before Angie could slide from her seat.

Angie stood beside her and closed the door. "Don't you think that's high up?"

She nodded, a smile glowing on her face. "But you can come with me."

"I don't think so, Carly." Rick's voice sounded behind them. "See the train. It has a slide, too, and look right over there. What do you see?"

"Swings." She eyed Rick. "You said I could go high on the swings. Can I?"

"I said I would push you." He took her hand, his promise causing a worry line on his brow. "Let's give the swings a try. Then we can decide."

"We have options." She tilted her head and looked at them with a grin.

Rick tried to cover his reaction, but Angie couldn't. Apparently Carly had learned a new word.

Angie followed them to the swings, noting only a few children were playing in the park. Since it was dinnertime and also getting later in the day, she suspected earlier in the afternoon the Playscape had been filled with children.

Rick helped Carly onto the swing's belt seat as she clutched the chains. A small push sent her sailing forward as she let out a squeal. "Higher, Daddy."

Angie caught Rick's questioning glance, but she only gave a one-shoulder shrug. Rick needed to make his own

decisions. Yet if she'd been really concerned, she would have verbalized it.

"Here goes. Hang on." Rick gave her a harder push, sending her farther into the air but not high enough to lose her balance. Her squeal frightened birds in the nearby trees, and as they watched them flutter through the sky their laughter joined Carly's.

Though she loved the swings, Carly's interest in the tower won out, and she wanted to head for the slides. Angie eyed the platforms, which featured an enclosed tube jutting from the top level perhaps sixteen feet high while an open slide, safer for Carly's age, projected from the lower level. A motherly instinct, only a hint at first, had grown into emotions she'd never expected. Carly was becoming more than Rick's little girl. She'd wheedled into Angie's heart and filled a hole she was startled that she'd kept hidden even from herself.

Angie smiled when Carly chose the safer slide, doing as her dad had said earlier. The girl scampered into the black-and-red train engine and glided down the small yellow slide for younger children. "Look at that. She minded you without a flinch," Angie said.

But at the bottom, Carly rose and eyed the second-level slide in the tower. "Can I go down that one?"

Rick shook his head. "This is the one for five-year-olds, Carly."

"Daddy, it's for babies. I'm almost six."

Angie pressed her lips together to control her laugh, softened by the expression in Rick's eyes. It touched her to see the love he had for Carly and the desire he had to keep her young. Sometimes she longed to have someone love her so unconditionally. Admitting her longing surprised her.

Rick slipped his arm around Carly's shoulders. "I think you're right, sweetie."

He followed her to the tower, and she climbed the stairs. A moment later she appeared at the top of the first slide platform. She waited for a child in front of her to come down, and on her turn she sat and zoomed to the bottom, landing safely. "See, I'm big enough."

"Definitely." He winked at Angie over his shoulder. "If you're careful you can play here for a while, and Angie and I will sit right over there at that table and watch. Okay?"

Carly didn't wait to answer. She shot up the stairs and slid down again while Angie's emotions swept her away. Was this how it felt to be married with children? The sense of having a loving family rolled through her.

Rick slipped his hand into Angie's and led her to the square table not far away where they could keep their eye on Carly without worry. His hand warmed hers and the feeling seeped into her chest. She loved watching Rick's interaction with Carly. Though she was a child, he gave his daughter a chance to express herself and treated her with a respect that she reciprocated. Children should respect their elders, but she'd witnessed some kids getting mouthy with parents as if they had a right. Teaching by example proved to be the successful way of helping children show manners and respect. That was how she'd been raised.

When she slipped onto the bench, Rick released her hand and joined her. In a moment, his arm slid behind her back and the same warmth seeped through her. He moved his fingers across her shoulder as gentle as a caress, arousing emotions she'd tried to avoid. Sensations rolled down her arm, tripped her pulse and awakened her longing.

Angie had never pictured herself raising children, not even one child. Yet today, once again, Rick's gentle touches

and Carly had opened the door wider. A child completed her in a way.

Values and beliefs, knowledge and truth ended with death, unless someone else could carry on the legacy. The thought startled her. She blinked, focused on the tower and the slide.

Carly shot down again, and Rick shook his head, seeming amazed. "She's having a wonderful time, Ang. Look, she's even made friends with that little girl." He raked his fingers through his hair. "I could kick myself for not taking her to a park or teaching her how to do things. I acted as I'd been raised. My dad worked long hours, my mom spent a lot of time volunteering at the church, and once I was old enough, I grew on my own, pretty much. Our family had dinners together most of the time. We went on a few vacations. Dad, on rare occasions, tossed me a baseball or helped me build a kite, but I did things with my friends mainly."

"My mom was hands-on." Recent phone calls validated her recollection. "As she is now. She kept an eye on our every movement. She read me stories when I was little. I remember that. But I had friends or played with kids in the neighborhood when I was young. Not much different from you."

He studied her a moment and seemed to want to ask a question, but he didn't.

"Rick, you're not alone."

He gave her shoulder a squeeze.

She turned to him, captured by the look in his eyes. "You've started me thinking about my faltering faith. Seeing your actions are putting cracks in my armor. I can't thank you enough. And Carly's opened doors for me, too, Rick. She's a lovely child despite all the problems you've faced with your marriage. She's a wise child, and she's

doing fine. Don't belittle what you've done. You're a won-
derful father."

His finger brushed her jawline while her heartbeat skit-
tered through her.

She caught her breath. "Love doesn't mean entertain-
ing a child. It means loving them. You show Carly respect
and give her protection and security. You guide her, and
you do what you know how to do. Buy pizza and read her
books. What's better?"

"The park?" His expression softened, and he shook his
head. "You've been an amazing teacher to me as well as
Carly, Angie. Who would have known this could hap-
pen." Rick's eyes captured hers again. He leaned closer
and kissed her cheek.

Her heart soared. Though she longed to dismiss the
amazing emotion, her feelings only deepened. She needed
to sort her thoughts, her priorities, her goals.

She needed time, period—time to see what life had in
store. Rick would say what God had in store, and maybe
there was something to that. To believe. It had been a long
time. With belief came hope, and that was what she had
been missing.

Though she longed to kiss him back, she only squeezed
his hand. "I suppose we should move closer before Carly
feels abandoned."

He shook his head. "Look at her. She's having a ball."
Nonetheless, he rose and they wandered back to the tower,
his hand brushing hers and her fingers itching to weave
through his and hang on forever.

On Monday evening Rick's phone starting ringing be-
fore he could prepare his dinner. When he heard it, an edgy
feeling crept through him. He checked the caller ID and

understood why: Glenda. He released a stream of air and grasped the receiver. "What's up, Glenda?"

Silence hung on the line a second. "I'm curious, Rick. Since Carly arrived home from after-school day care, I've heard nothing but Angie this and Angie that. What's going on?"

His lungs deflated. His head rocked on his shoulders as he struggled to find words that weren't bitter. "Nothing's going on."

"Really?"

Her brusque tone signaled his need to tread lightly. He should have expected it. Carly seemed captivated by Angie's fun-loving nature, and Carly seemed to know her feelings were reciprocated. But how could he explain it to Glenda?

Or did he need to?

"Rick? Are you there?"

"Yes. I'm trying to figure out what you want to know, Glenda. Ask me something I can answer."

"All right, who's Angie? And even more, why is Carly spending so much time with her. Is she your babysitter?"

"I've mentioned Angie to you before. I'm sure. She's a coworker who I've been helping with her move."

"How long does it take to move?"

"Glenda, please. Angie has been a friend for a long time. Yes, we're coworkers, and you know the company policy. We are only friends. She suggested I bring Carly over, and we took her to Bentley Park. They have swings and slides. That was our exciting day." He winced, admitting to himself it had been an amazing day.

"I don't want Carly exposed to any of your carousing."

He blew out another stream of air and rolled his eyes. "Have you known me to carouse, Glenda? And to be honest, you sound jealous."

"Jealous." Her pitch raised twenty decibels. "What are you talking about?"

"That's what I've been asking myself. What are you talking about? Glenda, please. Let's not grill each other for no reason. I understand. You want Carly in good hands, and she couldn't be in better. I'm her dad. I adore her just as you do. I have friends as you do. I occasionally see friends, and I'm sure you do, too. I don't call you every evening to find out who you talked with and what Carly was doing at the time. I don't accuse you of carousing if you spend time with someone and have fun. Please give me that respect."

"You always blow things out of proportion, Rick. All I want to know is that Carly is with you. That you're raising her and not dumping her off with someone else while you do your own thing."

"Never fear, Glenda. When I'm with Carly, she is my priority. I know you feel the same way."

He waited, listening, hoping for an apology, but none came.

"I have Carly next weekend, so enjoy yourself, Rick. I have some fun plans for Carly myself."

Now he understood. Angie was competition. "I'm glad. Carly loves having fun. If that's all, then, I'd like to eat dinner."

"That's all." She hung up.

He stared into space, hoping to figure out what he could do to smooth things over with Glenda. She had always been a bit suspicious, and he knew why. She'd been dumped by a louse before she'd met him. And now, as he thought about it, he probably had been her rebound solution, but it had gone too far. Marriage. He'd loved her. Glenda was bright and attractive, though a sense of humor wasn't her

strong point. She'd been more forward and pointed in her opinions.

He pulled himself from the phone call and headed for the kitchen for something to eat. He pulled out a frozen dinner, one of those healthy ones with small portions, but for now that would be enough. After checking the directions, he readied the container and popped it into the microwave. Then he put a K-Cup of strong French coffee in the brewer.

He sank onto a kitchen chair and reviewed the weekend. The feeling of being a couple permeated his thoughts. Though his feelings might be unwise, he had little control over his heart. Angie had always been special to him. She'd listened to his tale of woe and yet had never come on to him as some women had when they'd learned his marriage was falling apart. He'd been discreet, but information had leaked out no matter how careful he'd been.

Angie had been different. She'd listened and said little. Yet he sensed she cared. On occasion she would offer suggestions, providing ideas to work out his differences with Glenda and showing compassion when she watched his marriage fail. Wise. She'd been that way from the beginning, so why did her wisdom with Carly surprise him?

And what now? He'd let his feelings slip at the park. He'd kissed her. Only her cheek, but he'd seen in her eyes that she'd understood. She'd sensed his feelings. If only he could sense hers.

The microwave beeped, but he didn't move.

Angie sank onto the chair and unfolded the top of her lunch bag, her mind reviewing the awkward conversation with her mother. Again. No matter how she tried to sway the conversation, her mom veered it back to meeting the new man in her life.

Rick had become the man in her life but not as her mother suspected. Calling him a new man wasn't accurate. They'd been friends too long for that, but his offer to help with the move had made all the difference. They'd had time to really talk and laugh without the scrutiny of their fellow coworkers. He'd entered into her life as a friend and nothing more. His presence had grown beyond her expectations, beyond her imagination even. Now if she missed seeing him for one day, his absence caused her to feel as if she'd lost part of herself. Sometimes the feeling overwhelmed her.

Her mind in a haze, she looked up when she heard the lunchroom's door open. Rick strode in. He waved and headed for the refrigerator. She responded, but he seemed on a mission or distracted.

Only a day had passed, but it was strange how she had missed him. She'd seen little of him yesterday. She'd been involved in a meeting that had carried over her lunch break and thrown off her schedule. And Rick didn't always work in her area. Yesterday he'd probably been in a different department.

Rick dropped his lunch bag on the table and pulled out a chair. When he sat, he gave her a half smile. Stress seeped into the creases of his face. "Didn't get a chance to talk yesterday, did we?"

She shook her head, studying his face. "Is everything okay?"

Instead of responding, he flinched as if he preferred not to talk about it.

She shook her head. "So, you heard from Glenda?"

An audible sigh escaped him before he lifted his gaze. "You read me too well, Ang."

"What's going on? I hope it's not Carly. Is she sick?"

"No, she's great actually. She came home from school

on Monday, bubbling about all the fun she had with Angie. She told her mom about the park, I'm sure, although Glenda didn't talk about that."

Angie's heart compressed seeing Rick's misery. "Then what was it?"

"Apparently you."

"Me?" Her hand flew to her chest, startled at his answer. "Why? Did I do something wrong?"

"You know better than that, but I asked myself the same question for a fleeting moment and then realized that Glenda's jealous of you."

"Jealous? That doesn't make sense. Or does it?" She bit her lip. "You've mentioned she's a busy woman, works long hours and then comes home to Carly. I can picture her wanting time for herself but she can't if she's to spend time with a five-year-old." She pictured her in Glenda's shoes, but could only imagine the joy she would feel having Carly running into her arms and giving her a hug. Pure joy.

"I think you understand."

She nodded. "I can't relate to that no matter what, but I know Glenda and I are very different people. My ability to love is on the other end of the spectrum."

"You couldn't be more accurate."

As he shared the details of the conversation, she recognized Glenda's resentfulness, but then, could she blame her? A mother, no matter how she interacted with her child, wanted to be important in the child's life. What mother wanted to hear her child extolling the virtues of another woman and the fun she had with her? "How can you stop Carly from telling her mom what she does with you? It isn't right to ask her and, knowing Carly, she loves to talk about her experiences and wants her mom to be proud of what she's learned. I don't see an answer."

"I don't see one, either." He unwrapped his sandwich and took a bite.

A cold feeling ran through her veins. "Rick." Her pulse hitched as her solutions grew.

His worry-filled eyes sought hers. "What are you thinking?"

Shaking her head, she managed to steady her voice. "It might be best to lay low awhile. You've had fun seeing what Carly enjoys. Maybe for a few weeks Carly's weekends with you should be that. You and Carly." She closed her eyes a moment. "I think that could alleviate Glenda's anxiety. At least, I hope it would."

As her comment sank in, his face washed of color. "But…" He drew in a breath. "Angie, it's not only Carly that's having a good time. I hope you know that. I'm enjoying life far more than I have in years. Who knew what connection we would have away from the firm?"

His comment washed over her. She'd never guessed the difference it would make having him as a personal friend and not just a friendly coworker. She searched his eyes. "Should we try it for a while?"

His shoulders lifted and lowered again. "Let me think about it. But I can see where you're coming from. I don't need anything to put barricades between Glenda and me. It's hard on Carly. She senses it. The child's too intuitive."

Angie eyed her watch. "I should get back. I'm behind. Yesterday's meeting took a toll on my productivity."

He gave a single head nod. "Before you go, give me a brief summary of what's bugging you. Is it my situation? I don't think so. I noticed your look when I came in here."

She covered her face with her hands, wishing she could monitor her expressions. They seemed to reveal her concerns. "Nothing new. My mom called again. She insists she meet you, and she suggested this weekend. I tried to

wiggle out of it, but I'm about ready to be honest. Maybe she'll understand that I don't want to meet the nice guy who loves dogs or the bird-watcher who is shy but sweet. You have enough on your plate, Rick. I'll deal with it."

He held up his hand. "Wait a minute. We've gone out together with Carly. Isn't that a date? We wouldn't be adding to the lie."

Lie? "Can we call it being evasive? That sounds so much better."

Rick's face brightened more than it had since he'd arrived. "You can call it anything you want. What do you say? I don't have Carly this weekend, and I'd be happy to meet your mother."

"First, let's face facts. Talking of exaggeration, I don't think going to a park or a garden nursery is a date, so…"

"Then I have a solution."

His spirited tone caught her interest. "Okay, let's hear it." She couldn't help but grin.

"I read in the church bulletin last Sunday they're having an old-fashioned ice cream social on the church property with a few local praise bands as entertainment. Ours is great. Carly bounces to the music, and I do admit I've been known to tap my toe."

A laugh burst from her. "Not the old telltale toe-tapping."

He joined her, yet his expression let her know he was waiting for her answer.

"A date or not, that sounds like fun, and who can pass up ice cream?"

"With hot fudge, peanuts, whipped cream and a cherry on top."

She rose and slipped her chair against the table. "It's a date." Her heart in her throat, she hurried from the room and faced the truth. She had once again ignored her own warnings. What had happened to the idea of needing time?

Words spilled into her mind and she tried to sort them—
something she'd read in a college lit class. The seventeenth-
century essayist's quote had intrigued her then. Now it had
meaning. *Time, which strengthens friendship, weakens
love.* A chill prickled her spine.

Time. Did she really need it?

Chapter Five

Rick pulled two lawn chairs from the trunk and scanned the church lawn for a good place to watch the program. "How about there?" He motioned toward an open space not too far from the temporary bandstand.

"It looks okay to me," Angie said.

He maneuvered the chairs in one hand and Angie grabbed the small cooler bag. With his free hand, he guided Angie through the already crowded area. As they walked, he nodded to a few people he knew. He should have stopped to introduce Angie, but he'd failed to find the right words. "This is Angie, a coworker." She seemed so much more than that. "This is my friend Angie." But she'd become more than a friend. "My good friend Angie." Better. "I'd like you to meet Angie, the woman I'd like to spend my life—" His mind closed down, startled at the random thought that nonetheless felt real.

"Here we go." He propped a canvas chair against his leg while he unfolded the other and then finished the job. "Take this seat. It has a cup holder." She settled into it, and he took the cooler bag, set it on the ground beside him and flipped open the lid. "Pop? Cola or ginger ale? I think that's one you like."

She grinned. "Good memory. I rarely have soft drinks, but Vernors ginger ale is my favorite."

He popped open the can. "I have a paper cup in here."

"No need." She grinned. "This is fine."

He opened a cola and sank against the canvas chair back. "Are we set up for Sunday?"

"Royally." She rolled her eyes. "You're invited to dinner. I'm sure it will be a family event. My sister, Connie, wouldn't miss this."

Though he'd volunteered, he began questioning his wisdom. "You don't think they're expecting a wedding date, do you?" He managed a chuckle although his pulse did a skip. Wedding. It sounded wonderful, but the idea had yet to be anything more than a fantasy.

"You never know." She drew up her shoulders. "Talk in circles. That's what I do."

The first band began to set up onstage, and he hoped Angie would enjoy the music. It might encourage her to attend worship with him. Images billowed in his memory— Angie laughing at Carly's antics, Angie teaching her how to set a table, Angie hugging her with love in her eyes.

His chest constricted as each obstacle knocked him back. If anything good happened between them, he had to face his employers, Glenda and his attitude about being a mediocre father.

"You're thoughtful."

He raised his head and looked into Angie's eyes. "Sorry. My mind took off without me."

She chuckled and rested her hand on his. "We all have those strange moments."

"Hello, everyone! Welcome to our ice cream social and praise-o-rama."

The young man's voice belted over the speaker, and conversations faded.

"If you know the words to the songs, join in. If not, by the end of the song, you should know the chorus. If you're ready, let's sing the Lord's praises."

Applause echoed across the landscape as they began. "Let everything that has breath praise the Lord." When the audience picked up the melody and joined in, Angie followed. Her clear voice touched him, and gooseflesh bristled on his arms.

He gave her a fleeting smile and was immediately sorry since she softened her voice. Rick leaned closer. "I love hearing you." He joined in the praises with *I will worship you, I will worship*... The words lifted him higher and he soared when Angie joined in the final praises.

The song ended. His heart rejoiced for the special moment. "You know that song."

"I used to go to church when I was young. I drifted away after college. I don't even remember why."

From the expression on her face, he guessed she had an inkling, but this was no time to press her on that topic. The next song began. "Humble Thyself in the Sight of the Lord." His emotions replayed in the words: *he would be lifted up higher and higher.* It was what he'd felt. What he'd experienced.

Though Angie sang a few phrases, now she listened as if soaking in the words. He remained silent, enjoying the time together, yet longing to touch her soft skin, to hold her hand that rested on the chair's canvas arm.

Taking a chance, he placed his hand on hers, avoiding any action that might arouse her concern. When she shifted her eyes to his and smiled, he curled his fingers over hers and held his breath. What more could he ask for?

The first set ended. Before he could suggest they go check out the ice cream, Angie swung toward him, a serious expression on her face. "This music has brought back

so many memories, Rick. Really good memories of a time I was connected with my faith and when I knew Jesus was with me and I could lean on Him." She glanced away, and he watched her brush moisture from her eyes. "Such a simple thing, really. Faith is exactly that. Trusting. Hoping. Loving. How could I have walked away so easily?"

With his heart in his throat, Rick scuffled for words that would make a difference for her. "Evil is everywhere, Ang, always looking for a tiny chink in our beliefs. Temptations beguile us and we stumble away, looking for answered promises and something to delight us. We've all been there in our own ways." He touched her cheek. "And you're beginning to realize again what it is that really delights us. Our Lord."

She closed her eyes, emotions sweeping like a kaleidoscope across her face. "You just described my relationship with Cal. I was beguiled by a world I'd never known and promises he could never keep." She drew in a lengthy breath. "Thank you. I really understand what happened. I was deluded, deceived, enticed. No excuses. My strength failed me, a strength I prided myself on having."

"Ang, it's not hard to be fascinated by new experiences and blame ourselves for our weaknesses. Not long ago, you reprimanded me for calling myself a bad, maybe a mediocre, dad. Do you remember?"

A tender look touched her face, and she nodded.

"Do you remember what you told me?"

Angie slipped her hand around and wove her fingers through his. "I do. Thank you again. I need to listen to my own preaching." She leaned across the gap and kissed his cheek. "You're a wonderful man, Rick. The best."

The best. He had nothing to say that could capture what her words meant to him. He smiled and touched her cheek. His cell phone's ringtone began, and he let his hand drop.

When he eyed the caller ID, he saw Glenda's name. "What does she want now?"

"Rick, take the call."

His heart jumped realizing Glenda had used his cell phone. He hit the talk button, and his eyes widened hearing Carly's voice.

"Are you okay, sweetheart?"

"I had fun, Daddy."

"You did." He glanced at Angie, surprise still coursing through him. "What kind of fun?"

"Mommy took me to the Railroad Days, and I have a flower painted on my cheek, and I watched the clowns toss things in the air. And you know what?"

Her voice piped through the line and, hoping Angie could hear, he pulled the phone away from his ear. "No, what."

"They caught them."

"That's called juggling."

"Juggling. And they made animals and surprises with balloons. I have one, Daddy. Can I bring it to your house so you can see it?"

"You sure can." If it lasted that long. He pictured her disappointment when tomorrow they were airless pieces of rubber.

"And we got to go inside a capoose. It had a porch on it. It was so fun, and Mommy and I pretended we were going on a trip and waving goodbye."

Ah. Now he understood. "You were in a caboose."

"Uh-huh. A capoose."

He grinned and didn't correct her.

"And we had ice cream with chocolate and a cherry on top."

"I love ice cream sundaes, too. I think I'll have one today myself." He grinned at Angie and inclined his head toward the ice cream bar.

A smile brightened her face and warmed him.

"Mommy says I have to say goodbye now, Daddy. I love you."

"I love you, too, sweetheart." His knees weakened hearing his little girl's words. He loved her more than life. "I'm glad you called. Tell your mommy thank you for letting you call my cell phone." He rolled his eyes, making sure Angie saw him.

"I told her you might not be home. Are you?"

"No, I'm out, too, but not having as much fun as you are."

She giggled, and he heard her mother take the phone and end the call.

"I'm so happy Glenda's doing something with Carly. She needs to be the center of her attention sometimes. I know she's busy and tired, but—"

"But a mother needs to take time for her kids. They are her priority. I'm glad she's doing things with Carly and hope she's been motivated by hearing the fun things you and Carly have done."

He chuckled. "Jealousy can be powerful motivation for action. She's competing, Angie, and I'm glad. Whatever it takes, Glenda's being a mom." He shook his head. "I don't mean to belittle her. I too understand how difficult it is to be a single parent, but I know she is a good mother. She just needs to let Carly see that."

Angie touched his cheek, but the sweet smile on her lips faded. "On that note, I thought of something I meant to mention to you, and it's difficult to ask this." She lowered her eyes. "But it's only temporary."

An uneasy sensation crept up his back. "What is it?"

"When you visit my family, I think it would be wise not to talk about Carly. It will stir up issues, I'm afraid. I know my mom, and she could blow things out of propor-

tion. She always fears a man will take advantage of me. You know, like he needs a mother for his child, so he beguiles her into a marriage. That isn't love." She shook her head, her tension growing. "She rubs Cal in my face on occasion. She doesn't mean to do it, but…"

Her request dampened the joy he'd been experiencing with her. Yet he tried to understand. She made sense in a way. He'd seen her family hovering and wanting details of her every move, but still…

"I've hurt you, Rick, and I'm sorry. You know how much I love Carly, and I have to caution myself too not to talk about her. I want them to see you as the man you are and not look for an ulterior motive. Can I retract what I asked? You be who you are. That's a father of a lovely five-year-old daughter who means the world to me, too. Can you forgive me? I was stupid to ask this."

He reached for her hand. "Let's head over for an ice cream sundae. You don't need forgiveness. We have lots to talk about, and if they ask, I won't lie…or exaggerate, as you like to call it."

The comment made her laugh. "I don't want you to exaggerate or lie. You're Rick Jameson, Carly's dad, and if they want to find an ulterior motive, it won't bother me. I know the truth." She grasped his hand, and they headed for the ice cream bar as the next band began its first song, "Open the Eyes of My Heart, Lord."

The song struck home. Today assured him. He had to open the eyes of his heart. What was the point of lying about his feelings for Angie? Or exaggerating? He grinned. His feelings were real and growing.

When she heard the doorbell chime, Angie rested the broom against the doorjamb, her curiosity growing, and went to the door. As she approached the screen, she grinned.

"Elwood. El, how nice to see you." She unlocked the door and pushed it open. "Please, come in."

His eyes twinkled as they seemed to do. "I only wanted to tell you how great your landscaping looks with all the new flowers. Very pretty, and I see you've added some perennials."

"I did." She drew back again and pushed open the screen door wider. "But won't you come in?"

He pondered a second before he grasped the door frame and stepped into the foyer. "I don't want to trouble you. I'm sure Saturday is cleaning day." He grinned. "Or it seemed to be my wife's. I think her mother did it that way."

Angie chuckled. "I'm glad you came by. I made some cookies a couple days ago, and I have more than I need." She motioned toward the kitchen. "I want to send a few home with you."

"But what about that little girl I see here? I'm sure she enjoys—"

"Carly." She grinned. "She's Rick's daughter, and he only has her every other weekend. I promised when she's here again she could help me bake cookies." She winked. "She'll have plenty of cookies."

"You're going to teach her to bake. Good for you." He paused as curiosity spread across his face. "So he's widowed?"

Angie winced, fearing he might not approve of their friendship. "Not widowed." She looked away. "He's—"

El patted her arm. "No need to explain. He's divorced. It happens too often in this world even when one party is against it. Sad situation."

"He tried to keep it together, especially for Carly's sake, but she wanted her freedom."

"The story's familiar."

She motioned to an easy chair. He glanced behind him

and sat, and she took a seat near him. "I'm afraid we'll see that one of these days on Lilac Circle. I have too much time on my hands, I guess. Who'd think I'd be a nosy old codger? Pretty soon you'll be calling me Birdie." He shrugged. "I see too much sittin' out on the stoop."

"You mean Rema?" She feared he meant her neighbor. With her mind on Rick, she'd paid little attention to the happenings at Rema's.

He shrugged. "I fear so. That man of hers is gone more than he's there. Now, you can't tell me he works all those hours." He lowered his eyes. "Scripture says the tongue is a restless evil, full of deadly poison. I need some kneel time with the Lord. I'm old enough to know better than to gossip."

"El, you're not gossiping. And by the way, who's Birdie?"

"Ah, you haven't met her. I should keep my mouth shut." He swung his hand toward the redbrick house across the street where the road jogged. "She's the neighborhood hawk. She sees everything, and the good thing about it is if your home is ever burgled, she'll have a full description of the perpetrator and likely will have already called the police."

She chuckled. "You're kidding. I guess I haven't had the pleasure."

"I'm sure you will. She watches your house, you can be sure. Birdie gives us all a chuckle. She rarely does harm, but she lets you know what she thinks."

Meeting Birdie would be another experience she would face when it happened. "But talking about what someone thinks, I think you're as far from a gossip as one can get. Gossips are usually focused on stirring up trouble. You're a godly man with no malice in your heart."

"Thank you." He gave her a subtle nod, yet seemed unconvinced.

"El, you know I care about Rema and so do you. We're concerned for her. Thanks for letting me know what you suspect. I need to be a better friend." Her mind flew to Rick, who'd been the best friend in the world, and what had she really done for him?

"Thank you. I do feel sad for her, and I've never spoken to anyone but you. You seem special, Angie. I've seen you a bit with that little girl, and I shook my head and said that woman should be a mother. You're a natural."

Her cheeks warmed. "I never thought I'd be a mother. I still have no plans, but I've enjoyed getting to know Carly. She's a special child. Wise for her years."

"Don't close your eyes to motherhood, Angie. The Lord has our best at heart. Have you heard the scripture, a man plans his course, but the Lord determines his steps? It's not only a man. You can change that to a woman plans her course." He gave her a wink.

She grinned, tickled by his humor.

"I think that's what you've done. You've planned your course." He chuckled, his eyes twinkling. "But the Lord will guide you. Just open your heart."

His words triggered her memory. The song filled her mind that she'd heard at the ice cream social with Rick. "Do you know this song, El?" She began to sing, "Open the eyes of my heart, Lord."

El joined in, his rich baritone affected by only a small tremor.

The joy on his face stirred her, and a sensation awakened something inside the depths of her being. When the song ended, she rose and gave Elwood a hug. "El, you have a really good voice. I love that song."

"I did have a voice once before I sounded as if I was sittin' on a washing machine." He slapped his lap and rose. "Now it's time to let you get back to work." He rose,

stood a moment to get his balance and then stepped toward the doorway.

"Not before I ask you a question and give you some of those cookies." A few cookies could never repay for the moment that a door had opened inside her as if someone in a dark room had turned on the light.

El looked at her with question.

"The question first. I know how the street got its name, but who conspired to have everyone on the street to plant lilacs?"

He chuckled. "Well, now, that's not a difficult question at all. One Fourth of July we had a block party. Everyone shared food for a potluck, and we sat along the street swapping stories." He leaned back and looked up as if thinking.

"So someone mentioned it as a street project."

El shook his head. "Not quite. A neighbor said he'd purchased a couple of lilac shrubs to plant in his backyard, and someone else popped up and said he'd been thinking the same thing." He slapped his leg with a chuckle. "Pretty soon someone else liked the idea, and not to be outdone, soon the whole bunch of us had decided to plant the shrubs. That's it in a nutshell."

Angie grinned, thinking it was a pretty big nutshell.

El took a step toward the door. "I've taken enough of your time, so—"

"No, you don't." Angie held up her hand. "Not until you get those cookies." She hurried into the kitchen. She dropped cookies into a plastic bag and carried them back to El, who was standing by the door. "Thank you for the visit and for reminding me to visit Rema. She needs to know I care." She handed him the bag of cookies. "These are for you. And I hope you know I care about you, El. You have

a way of opening my eyes with the right words at the right time. You've given me food for thought."

His eyes crinkled. "And you've given me food for my sweet tooth." He patted her arm, opened the door and made his way down the steps and out to the public sidewalk. As he turned to head home, he gave her a wave. She waved back, sensing she was different than she had been when he'd arrived at her door.

Rick scanned the faces eyeing him. Angie had been right. Each family member studied him in their own way, either with hope or with eagerness to prove their relationship was useless. Her mother's face glowed with expectation, as if searching for a clue to his romantic intentions. Her sister's brown eyes snapped with suspicion, letting him see what Angie had been up against.

As they sat in her mother's homey living room, he sensed their underlying attempt to analyze everything he said and did. He pressed his back into the overstuffed chair. Even the flowery upholstery did not give him a comfy feeling. Aware of their scrutiny, he plastered on a pleasant look, not wanting to upset Angie. She'd worried enough about spending the Sunday afternoon with them.

"So, you met at work."

His sister's expression held doubt.

"We did. I had already been there for a few years when Angie joined us. Since we were in the same department then, I took her under my wing, and we got to know each other."

"But now?" Her mother's eyes bored through him, even though she'd planted a smile on her lips.

"Now? I'm in a different department most of the time, but..." He glanced at Angie, at a loss for words.

"Mom, I told you. Rick and I are very good friends.

We enjoy each other's company and we've done some things together outside work. He was a great help when I moved."

Rick chuckled. "She learned if I could do nothing else, I was great at lugging boxes up the stairs."

Her dad arched a brow. "I'm sure you have other talents." His brow belied his grin.

"Yes, Dad." Angie's tone held an edge. "This man can eyeball a picture hanger so it lies perfectly straight on a wall. I don't own a lever."

"Level." Rick tried to cover his laugh, but her father got the humor, and for the first time, Rick felt some camaraderie with her dad.

Her father slapped his leg. "I guess this is why I need a son." He winked. "For self-defense." Her father rose and gave a head toss. "Let me show you my tool shop, Rick. You might appreciate it."

"I know I will." He rose, aware that he'd stretched the truth. The last thing he wanted to do was be cornered alone with her father.

Her father motioned for him to follow. They went through the kitchen still filled with the rich scents of the roast and baked vegetables. He had to admit that Mrs. Bursten was an excellent cook.

Angie's dad led him into the backyard and to a small building attached to the garage. When her father opened the door, Rick stepped inside and faltered. "Mr. Bursten, this is cleaner than my kitchen."

"Call me Tom, and thank you. Tools are friends, and we treat friends well. Get me?"

"I do." He pointed to the peg board wall filled with his tools. "And I see you have a level." He gave Tom a wink. "Or lever, as your daughter likes to say."

Tom shook his head. "I used to teach her a few things out

here, but I don't suppose we ever used a level. She knows how to change a tire and change her oil." He shrugged. "I hope she remembers."

"I'm sure she does. She's told me you raised her right."

Her dad, a slender man with only a slight midlife paunch, hung his head. "And that leads me to my real reason for bringing you out here." He lifted his chin and looked into Rick's eyes. "I want to apologize for my wife and my daughter. Rose and Connie got a bad gene from somewhere in the family. I hope Connie's wasn't from me."

Rick wanted to chuckle from nerves and the man's wit, but he stopped himself.

"Sometimes I think those two women look for the negatives in everything rather than the positives. You don't deserve that." Tom grasped Rick's arm and gave it a shake. "I've only known you for an hour or so, but I can see you're a nice man." He added a wink. "And I can see the way my daughter looks at you. If she likes you, and she does, then so do I."

He extended his hand and Rick grasped it with a firm shake. Tom was being open, and Rick liked that in a person. Angie took after her dad. "Thank you, sir. I think Mrs. Bursten worries about Angie being single. For many years, marriage was perceived as the goal of every woman, but in this world today, many women value their independence. I see that in Angie, and she's like you. She's open and puts the best construction on most everything."

"That's my girl." He seemed to study Rick's face for a moment. "I like you, and I'm glad you're a good friend to my daughter. If your feelings ever grow, I'd like that, too."

Heat rose up Rick's neck, and he hoped her father didn't have a keen eye for reading the truth. His feelings already had blossomed. They didn't have far to go to burst into a flower. The thing holding him back was having no idea

what Angie's feelings were. And yes, her weakened faith was a concern, yet he trusted the Lord that planting a seed gave hope of growth.

Tom waved him toward the doorway, and in moments, they were climbing the steps to the kitchen. Angie, he was sure, had been grilled by her mother and sister from the moment he'd vanished through the archway.

"If you're not serious about each other, then I still don't understand why you can't date someone else." Connie, with eyes as sharp as an eagle's, stood over her like a police sergeant. Even her slender frame and shapely curves couldn't waylay the image.

"Connie." Angie fought to keep a growing scowl from her face. "Because I am not interested. Can't you understand? I'm happy the way my life is. I don't want to meet a nice guy, no matter what he looks like or does for a living, or even if he has a great hobby. And most of all I don't want to jeopardize my relationship with Rick." She rose, fighting back a scream. "Why can't you understand? I am not interested."

Connie backed up a foot, her eyes wide and dazed. "I didn't—"

"We're back, ladies." Her father's voice severed Connie's response, and all eyes rose to watch her dad and Rick come through the archway and sit down.

She knew immediately that Rick had heard part of the conversation, and her heart sank. What good was dragging him here in their pretense? Her sister, even more than her mother, would not understand.

Sinking back into a chair, she managed to fake a pleasant look, but Rick's expression told her he'd read right through it.

Connie huffed from the room, and her mother rose, ten-

sion etching her face. "I think it's time for dessert." Her mom hurried off behind Connie.

Angie wanted to sink into the cushions and vanish. She'd known the visit would include some grilling but not this way. The deep drilling into her intentions she expected, but not their inability to accept or at least understand her feelings. To them, her feelings didn't seem to count. She'd been accustomed to her mother's overbearing ways when she'd been a child and teen. Loving and caring caused moms to do that, but now that she'd turned thirty-three, the conversation had become unpleasant echoes from her past.

She slid to the edge of the chair, gathered her plan. "Dad, I know Mom made a special dessert, but I'm not really hungry and I think we should leave." She turned to Rick, her eyes probing his to understand what she had in mind.

"Angela." Her father's voice sounded weighted with concern. "Your mom doesn't mean to—"

"Dad, that's not it." She winced hearing another of her exaggerations. "Rick has—"

"Angie, don't speak for me." Rick's stern tone startled her. "I'm fine. Your mom made a dessert for our visit, and I would like to stay and enjoy it."

His eyes flashed an emotion she couldn't read, but it bored into her mind and her decision. "It's up to you, Rick."

She sank against the chair back and bit the inside of her lip. "I'm sorry, Dad, but you know Connie and—"

"I do, kiddo. I do. She and your mom were cut from the same cloth, I fear. You got your old dad's way of thinking and reacting, which isn't necessarily a good thing either, but—"

"I make mistakes, too, Dad." She cringed seeing her father's discomfort. "You're the best dad in the world, and I wouldn't trade you for anything. Please don't blame yourself." She turned to Rick. "And I'm sorry, Rick, that you've

been put under their scrutiny, too. It doesn't make for a pleasant afternoon."

"Your dad and I had a great visit, Angie. It's been great getting to know him." He smiled, and she recognized his sincerity.

"Thanks, Rick."

"You two are making me blush." Her dad gave a chuckle. "Or else it's getting warm in here."

She laughed.

Rick joined her and pulled out his cell phone. "It's eighty-four degrees outside, sir."

"Who's this 'sir' guy?" Her dad looked over his shoulder, his playfulness in full swing. "If you're talking to me, son, I'm Tom. Remember?"

Rick chuckled. "Right, Tom."

Their smiles faded when Connie plodded into the room. "Mom has dessert ready in the dining room." She arched her eyebrow. "She made her microwave chocolate pudding cake, which I haven't seen her make in years, even though I've begged."

Rick rose and took Angie's hand as she stood, and they followed her dad into the dining room aware that even the pudding cake had caused a cleft between her and her sister. Connie could make Mount Everest out of an anthill. Today was an obvious example, but Rick had squeezed her hand, reassuring her that he understood.

At least someone in her life did. Two people, really. Her dad always comprehended her meaning and her logic. He'd said they were alike, and in many ways they were. She was grateful for that.

Chapter Six

Rick pulled from the Burstens' driveway and waved at her parents hanging out the front door. Though he'd been welcomed, he sensed strain between Angie and her sister, and it bothered him. He disliked seeing Angie tense. Yet he needed to know more before he could understand what caused it.

With Angie's silence, he knew better than to ask. Once they were down the road he tried to find something to say to ease the strain. "Are you as full as I am? That dessert was delicious."

"I gave you an out." She kept her eyes facing the windshield.

Juggling what to do, he chose honesty. "You're angry at me for making us stay. I'm sorry, Angie. I—"

"I'm angry at myself, Rick. The 'out' was for me more than you. For some reason, Connie was in rare form. She's nosy, but I've never seen her so rigid in demanding my answers."

He tossed his question around a moment. "What answers?"

"Why I wouldn't accept a date from someone else if we didn't have a commitment. I'm not sure if Connie's

marriage is a happy one or not, but if it was I would think she would understand that a spoken commitment isn't the end-all of everything. The heart might be committed."

Her comment caused his pulse to skip. Was she talking about them or just people in general? He drew in a quiet breath and gave her comment thought. "I agree, Ang. The heart commits, but we make decisions based on two things—heart and mind. Sometimes logic overrides emotion."

She finally looked at him. "You really comprehend what I'm saying. Thank you. I wondered if I'd been talking gibberish."

"You made good sense. Though our hearts skip in our chests and our pulses race, sometimes our minds caution us to think things through. We look for possible problems, all the what-ifs and maybes. Then we don't know which way to turn."

She remained quiet, and though he wanted to blabber on just to keep sound in the air, he waited.

Time ticked by, and his edginess grew. Finally Angie manipulated her seat belt and shifted toward him. "I've been thinking. When you say it that way, it sounds empty. Thoughtless."

"When I say what?"

"You said we look for possible problems, all the what-ifs and maybes. That seems hopeless. If we care about a situation or a person, why would we look for something that isn't? Why not look for something that can be?"

His heart jumped. But he couldn't admit to her what was in his heart, and saying anything else sounded as if he didn't care. "It's the difference between the half-empty and half-full glass, Ang. That's how I see it."

She took time pondering his analogy. "It's the difference between looking at life in a positive way or negative way."

"You could say that."

"Talk about being full. You've given me something to think about. I was talking about Connie, but I see myself, too. It may take time but it's time well spent."

His heart rose to his throat. Her words gave him hope. His spirit lifted as an idea sparked in his mind. They needed quality time. Time alone. "What do you say we work off some of that pudding cake and go for a walk?"

She eyed him a moment. "A walk would be nice."

He pictured her mind weighing the idea.

Angie chuckled. "Yes, you're right."

His head jerked toward her, but he swung his face to the highway. "Glad I'm right, but I hadn't said anything."

"Sure you did. I saw your expression. You knew I was looking for the negatives of why not to go."

He grinned. "Guilty, sort of. I knew you were weighing the options."

"Let's go. I can use some exercise, and a walk sounds good."

He took the highway only a few miles from downtown and slipped into a parking spot at DeVries Nature Conservatory. He hurried around to open her door, but she'd already slipped out. Independent. He seemed to forget. He grinned and took her arm as he steered her toward the West Woods Trail. "Have you been here before?"

She shook her head. "Never. I've seen little here. I wanted a town not too far from work. I noticed the houses were well priced in Owosso. I found one I liked on Lilac Circle, and here I am."

He motioned to the building they were passing. "This is the Historic Carriage and Sleigh Museum. The trail we want is this way." He slipped his hand from her arm and captured her fingers in his.

She gave his hand a squeeze, sending his pulse kicking

its heels along his arm. Emotions were ridiculous at times, but he had little control.

They took West Woods Trail, and when they reached the floodplain path, he turned and followed it along the Shiawassee River. The sun dappled the ground with light and shadows while highlights glinted in Angie's hair as they walked in silence.

She slowed, and he measured his steps with hers. When she stopped, he paused beside her, looking at the water slipping over rocks and wending its way to the Saginaw River.

"It's so peaceful here, Rick. I don't want to let my family stress me, but I think I walked through the door with my what-ifs polished and ready for battle, and it happened. I can't continue to react to my sister's nagging about my being single or my mom's moaning about how much she wants a new grandchild."

His first thought was Carly. Her family would have a built-in grandchild if he and Angie... He stopped himself. Now he was also grasping at what-ifs. He needed to stay positive and hopeful. "You'll work it out. Take a long breath before you respond from now on. Ask yourself what would be the best answer to stop them." He chuckled. "I came to the conclusion once that if you agree with them, they can't argue."

"Agree? I don't get it. How can I agree if she's wrong?" Her face skewed with her question.

"For example, if Connie says you're wasting your life, you can answer 'yes, I guess I am.'"

Angie's eyes widened. "That would confuse her." She shook her head. "I do the opposite. I tend to defend myself."

"You'll enjoy catching her off guard. I've used that technique, even on the job, and it works every time."

A smile grew on her face. "I can't wait. Maybe I'll call her and apologize for hurting her feelings today. Then I can test it."

"Okay, but you don't need to be vindictive."

She broke into a laugh. "I won't. I promise." She took a step forward, and he captured her hand again as they walked in silence. Twigs cracked beneath their feet, and the soft sound of the river flowing beside them became their soothing melody. His hope grew.

As they turned to head back, he paused. "Let's sit a minute." He motioned toward the lone bench ahead.

She eyed it and nodded.

He settled beside her and tried to focus. "What do you hear, Ang?"

She tilted her head in concentration. "Birds. Do you hear how they call and then from the distance the same call is echoed back. They're talking, and I bet they understand each other." A grin swept over her face.

He knew the reference addressed her sister's lack of understanding. "I think they do."

"And I can hear the river and a bee." She leaned forward and brushed something at her hair. "It's gone." She leaned forward again as if concentrating on sound, but when she turned, he suspected her mind had been focused on her family. "I hear peace. Do you know what I mean?"

He didn't speak, only gave a nod as he slipped his arm along her back and rested his hand on her shoulder. "Peace like a river."

"That's a beautiful thought, isn't it?"

"It's in the Bible, and it's also in a hymn or a song. I've heard it." Rick dug into his mind, trying to remember where he'd heard those words that had made such an impact on him.

"You know a lot about music and faith, Rick. I envy you. I wish—"

"You can have it, too. When you read scripture or hear music, let the words sink in. If it means something, it will stick. I don't purposely memorize. I just retain what I've heard. You're a smart woman, Angie. You've just had a minor slip from faith, I think."

She lifted her hand and stroked his cheek, sending sparks through his chest. "I think so, too, and you've helped me take a new look. I feel different."

So did he, and without stopping himself, he leaned closer and his lips touched hers. His heart swelled, and to his joy, Angie grazed her fingers along the hair to the back of his neck and kissed him back. He eased away, longing to linger against her soft lips but not wanting to upset her.

Their eyes met, and they gazed at each other in silence as the birds called and the river rippled nearby, nature's melody leaving him with a song in his heart. He marveled at his rare poetic thoughts, but he knew the moment would live in him forever.

Angie paced her living room, stopping for a moment to stare at her cell phone on the lamp table. Then she turned to pace back across the room. Yesterday had been a roller-coaster ride. Emotions had spiraled through her body, looping along the path to ecstasy and then sinking to the pits of despair.

The kiss hung in her mind, spreading the beauty with guilt that she'd not only let it happen but had plunged into it. Enjoyed it. Wanted it. Falling for Rick had not been her plan. She'd fought it since she'd faced all the ramifications: her job, her independence, her lifestyle and her past. Rick believed everyone was a sinner but for the glory of God. She remembered that from her Sunday-school background,

too, but when they were her sins, her morals plummeting, her knowing what she was doing but not caring, she could never tell Rick the truth, forgiven or not.

But what she wanted and what she felt plowed off in two different directions and her control failed. Head and heart. They'd talked about it yesterday. Already she'd sunk back into the rut of the half-empty glass, the what-ifs, the negative.

Along with the emotional struggle, she missed Carly. The sensation was new. The little girl at first had been a fun addition to her life, but now everything felt different. She wanted to share her time and love with the child. Guilt hit her again as she recalled her request not to mention Carly to her family. Rick had complied, but she'd cheated him out of talking about the most important part of his life.

Her sister's barraging her with questions and her mother's hovering with her own curiosity had made her tension grow and Rick had spotted it. He always did. And he'd overheard the conversation, or part of it, with her sister. The tirade that had ended the afternoon with a knot in her stomach.

Worst of all, she'd avoided Rick all day at work. Facing him after the kiss seemed impossible.

She paused at the front window and looked out at the sky as sunlight hung low and reflected coral and gold along the horizon. She wanted to call Rick and apologize, talk, but her courage wavered.

Rema's front door swung open. Trey darted from the house, jumped into his car and squealed away. Something was wrong, but what? Her chest tightened fearing Rema had been injured or… Her concern swept away when she spotted Rema closing the front door.

She'd meant to drop by her house and see how she was doing. Now Angie pondered if today was a day she could be of help. Or maybe she'd blown the scene out of propor-

tion. Her own concerns fled as she grasped her cell phone, dropped it into her pocket and stepped outside.

As she crossed the street, she faltered a moment, trying to decide if her action was a good one or a bad choice. Whichever, she pushed herself forward and rang Rema's bell.

The door flew open, and Angie wanted to run. Rema looked at her, eyes red-rimmed and glassy with tears that clung to her lashes.

Rema pushed open the screen door and waved her in. Though Angie hesitated, she stepped forward, already having made the decision to visit despite the situation she'd witnessed. "I've come at a bad time, Rema. Maybe I should—"

Rema closed the door behind her. "No time's a good time anymore, Angie. Please come in."

Angie followed her into the living room and sat on the edge of an easy chair, telling herself to be more discerning when she made choices. "I saw Trey fly out of the house and, for a moment, I thought something had happened to you. I was relieved when I spotted you closing the door."

"In a broad sense, something did happen to me. I've had enough."

Biting the inside of her lip, Angie monitored her question, and without asking, she sensed she knew the answer. Enough of Trey's carousing. "Can I help? If nothing more, Rema, I can listen."

"I blinded myself for years, Angie. Not really blinded, but turned my head and didn't say a word."

Rema closed her eyes and remained silent, and for once, Angie did the same.

"Trey's long work hours and numerous weekend business ventures fooled me for a while, and though he paid the bills and tried to cover his expenditures, I found them and saw meals for two, massages for two, tickets for two." She

closed her eyes as she released a poignant sigh. "I wasn't one of the two, obviously. I sat home, lonely, bored, wishing his job didn't take him out of town so often. But finally, I took off the blinders and faced the truth."

"I'm sorry, Rema. I can't imagine…" Words failed her. She rose and wrapped her arm around Rema's shoulders and held her as she wept. Rema's tremors ebbed, and when she lifted her head, her soft voice sent sorrow down Angie's spine.

"I haven't been hugged in years. Trey dashed in and out, complained about my restlessness at night and slept in the guest room, and all but removed me from the house. Yet he stopped me from getting involved in activities, so I could fill my boredom with something worthwhile."

"You mentioned that a while ago."

"I haven't really talked to you since I decided to take a yoga class. One night after we were done, one of the women suggested we go out for dinner since we'd both skipped eating before the class. Though I worried about what I'd do if Trey came home and I wasn't here, I was brave and we went to a café not too far from the fitness center."

Watching Rema's expression, Angie surmised what had happened.

"We were seated at a small table away from the door, and for some reason, I looked up during our meal and almost choked."

"Trey was with someone."

"Right. She was an attractive woman, dressed in a tight outfit with a neckline that left little to the imagination. As they followed the hostess toward the back of the café, he held her hand. I could see the look on his face and wanted to die."

"Rema, no. Never say that. You wanted to live a life

of fulfillment as he seemed to be doing. You'd have been stifled and—"

"Held prisoner in a way." She shook her head. "Believe it or not, Angie, one time I was a fairly vibrant woman. I had dreams and plans, but Trey wanted a wife who would stay home and take care of the family—him and the children I never had."

"I don't understand. Do you mean you could never have children? And if not, are you sure it's you? Maybe Trey's the one with the problem."

Her eyes widened as if she'd never considered the possibility.

"I didn't mean to startle you, but often women assume the problem is theirs and it can very easily be the husband. Did you have tests and—"

"No. Trey said no."

Her brusque response threw Angie off kilter. "And that was it."

Rema nodded, averting her eyes.

Possibilities filled Angie's mind. Trey may have known he couldn't have children from the beginning. She shifted her gaze to Rema. "What will you do now?"

"I confronted him when he came home to change his clothes for another meeting." She dragged air through her lungs, her head rocking from side to side. "Meeting. Shmeeting. I'm tired of his lies. I've been made a fool, and now I wonder how many people knew about this and just haven't said anything. I could be the laughingstock of—"

"Don't think that way. No one of value would laugh at you. I'm sure people avoid telling the wounded party, but they're not laughing. They're more likely sick."

"Do you think so? Really?"

She sighed. "I would be. If I'd witnessed him with someone, I doubt if I could have told you, but I would probably

do something to steer you in that direction to investigate. You know, give you the momentum to investigate."

"Truthfully, I knew. The blinders made it insubstantial."

"But now it's real, Rema. I can only hope…pray that you find a solution."

"I will. It will be what I should have done years ago. I'll give him an option to either be a faithful husband or leave. Maybe then he'll give it a second thought and things will be different."

Angie heard the words but didn't believe it any more than Rema did from the expression on her face. Angie rose and drew Rema into her arms. "If you need me, I'm right across the street."

"Thank you. I wanted to come over a couple days ago while I was trying to decide what to do, but I knew I had to make the decision on my own."

Angie stepped toward the door. Dusk had fallen, and she needed to breathe. Rema's sadness had wrapped around her own confusion and weighed her down. "Just call or come over."

Rema nodded as Angie stepped onto the porch. She waved and crossed the street, recalling her own struggle with Cal and their different lifestyles and dreams. Though not married, they had lived together as if a married couple. She'd envisioned it would become a real marriage and that had helped wash away her guilt, but Cal's death ended her plan. The memory dampened her spirits. A time when she tossed her values and upbringing into the ditch had turned into a nightmare as far as it could get from the kind of dream she'd longed for.

Before she opened the door, her cell phone rang, and her mother's ID showed on the screen. "Mom."

A sob split the line, and Angie shrank into a child again,

knowing she'd hurt her mother. She pushed open her door and sank into the nearest chair. "Mom, what's wrong?"

Her mother described her father's lecture to her and Connie about pushing their desires on Angie, and as she listened she wanted to run into Rick's arms and hear his wise solutions to the problem.

"It wasn't your fault, Mom. I need to be less ready to jump on everyone. I came there expecting the battle between my wants and Connie's. And your desire for another grandchild. Please forgive me."

"Angie, I always forgive you no matter what. We're wrong not to listen to you. We just don't understand why you want to stay single and why—"

"Listen, Mom. I've never said I wanted to remain single forever. Marriage and children have not been part of my thoughts for a long time, but—"

"Not since Cal. Am I right?"

"Yes, you're right." Rick's solution came to mind. "But life is changing and I need time to sort through my thoughts. Pressure doesn't help me think clearly. You don't want me to marry without love, do you?" She thought of Rema's sad situation. "You and Dad have a faithful, devoted relationship. One I've admired over the years, and I—"

"You've admired us, Angie? I had no idea, and I understand that you want love before marriage. It's Connie who thinks that you can't find love if you're not dating and meeting people who are marriageable."

"But I am dating. Rick and I have a wonderful friendship, and friendships can grow deeper and become something more than just friends. But I get the feeling you and..." She swallowed. "It's my feelings that are significant, Mom, not Connie's or yours. Do you understand? We have the work issue that has been a blockade, but I think we've both dis-

missed that. If they want to do something about it, there are other places to work."

"Oh, Angie, I'm so happy. So you and Rick have talked about it. Then that means—"

"You jumped ahead of me again. No, we haven't discussed it, but I can tell how we feel, and that isn't as much of a problem. Give me time, Mom. That's all I need."

"I feel lots better, Angie. I thought you'd never want to come over again, and I thought Rick was a nice man. Your dad seems to think he's a keeper." She tittered. "That's what he called him."

"Dad has good taste, and one day I may have a surprise for you." Carly's face blossomed in her mind. "But don't hold your breath. I said time. That's what I need."

"Thank you, sweetheart. I feel so much better."

"I'm glad, and thanks for calling. I'd been thinking about calling you, too." But mostly she wanted to talk to Rick. Her pulse skipped as she recalled the gentle touch of his lips and her eager response. She couldn't deny it. She'd wanted his kisses for so long, but had denied it to herself.

Chapter Seven

When Rick arrived home on Tuesday, his phone rang again before he could open the refrigerator to decide what he would have for dinner. He checked the caller ID, expecting it to be Glenda, but instead he saw his parents' phone number. "Mom?" He sank onto a kitchen chair, anticipating a long call.

"Ricky, I didn't expect you to be home. I planned to leave a message and tell you Rene is coming for a visit. I figured you'd want to know."

His sister. He blew out a stream of air. "It's been a while, hasn't it? Is anything wrong?" She'd had a tense marriage for a while, but as far as he knew, everything was great now.

"Why would you think that? She has a few days off during the week. They're closing down the agency for an upgrade on their computers or something, so she's getting time off. She said they decided it best to work with only a skeleton crew."

He'd love time off with pay. "I'll have to come by and see her, or maybe she'd like to come here. I don't think she's seen this apartment, and maybe I could pick up Carly for a few hours to visit with her."

"How nice. I'm sure she'd love to see Carly. And so would Grandma."

"I know, Mom. For a while you were doing so much babysitting, I thought you'd had enough." He chuckled, knowing how she would respond.

"Me? I'd take that girl in a moment if you'd give her up."

"Not on your life, Mom. Maybe one day I'll come over with a friend of mine and bring Carly, too. I recently met her parents, and we—"

"Ricky." Her pitch rose. "Are you telling me this is serious? Are you thinking of getting—"

"Right now she's a friend, but I think you'd like her, and she adores Carly."

"Who doesn't? Anyway, I'm glad I caught you. You know I don't like to use that other phone of yours, Ricky. You might be in a meeting or—"

"If it's important, call." He shook his head. His mom had no idea about the work world or cell phones. "Don't worry about that. I would call you back as soon as I could if you called at an inconvenient time."

"Okay, if you're sure, but today I just wanted to leave a message. Rene should be here tonight, and I'll have her give you a call so you can make plans. And I'd love to meet your lady friend."

The way his mother said "friend" had a definite lilt to it. "Great, Mom. Talk later." When she disconnected, he chuckled. Ricky. He'd outlived that name to the world but not his mom. Angie would never let him live it down.

Angie. He closed his eyes, reliving the kiss they'd shared. He'd been unsure how she would react to it, but he'd longed to kiss her that way for too long, and he'd had to try.

Angie's response had been far more amazing than he had anticipated. She'd seemed as eager as he was. Except... He hadn't seen much of her since Sunday. She hadn't eaten

lunch when he did, and today she had been leaving when he'd walked into the lunchroom. She'd stopped a moment to say she'd talked with her mom and all seemed well, but other than that she'd given him a fleeting smile and headed back to her desk, leaving him clueless.

His head spun with questions. Was she sorry for the kiss, sorry for her reaction or afraid of where the kiss might lead? How would he know without asking her? And he couldn't do that.

He wanted to call her, but he also wanted her to call him. He'd feel more confident that everything was okay between them. His indecision wavered.

When his stomach rumbled, he rose and headed for the refrigerator. Nothing looked appetizing, but he settled for a sandwich and a bowl of canned soup. He never claimed to be a gourmet cook. He chuckled and the sound lifted his spirits. Before sitting down, he grabbed the newspaper from the living room, said a blessing and opened his mouth to take a bit of his ham and cheese on wheat. Instead, the house phone jarred him again. He lowered the sandwich, this time sensing the call was from Glenda.

When he looked at the caller ID, he grimaced. "What's up, Glen?" Glen? How long had it been since he'd called her that?

"I want to give you a heads-up and ask a favor."

Favor. That caught his attention. "Okay, shoot."

"I've been told that I may have to take another business trip, and I need to take care of some business on Thursday and Friday, so could you take Carly the extra days? She can stay longer at day care after school, and you could pick her up on the way home from work."

Tension filled her voice and he wanted more details about the trip, but asking now would only cause problems.

"No problem, Glenda. I'm always happy to have extra time with Carly. Where are you going on the trip?"

She remained silent and he continued to wait.

Finally she released a sigh. "Europe. Germany."

"Germany?"

"Yes, and I'm getting a passport for Carly."

The words rushed from her mouth and charged through him. "For Carly? Why?"

"I'd like to take her to experience another country, Rick. Wouldn't that be a nice experience?"

"Not if you're working, Glenda. She'd miss school and who would take care of her while you're—"

"I'll take care of that, Rick. It's not your problem."

Fire rose up his neck. Not his problem? "You're talking about Carly. She's our daughter. Yours and mine. So it is my problem, too." His stomach hitched. "How long are you talking about, Glenda? A week? It's hardly worth taking her for a week since you'll be busy."

Again she didn't speak, but he heard her breathing.

"You're talking about more than a week, aren't you? How long, Glenda?"

"I'm not sure. If I were I'd let you know."

"You certainly will, Glenda. I have a say in where Carly goes if it's out of state."

"Come on. Don't be a child. Would I do anything to hurt Carly?"

"Not intentionally. And before I say more, I'm no more a child than you are, Glenda. We're both adults and we need to act like adults. Would you want me to announce to you that I'm making plans to take Carly away to Europe for a few weeks? Maybe a month?" Maybe many months. He sensed something going on with Glenda. His hand trembled, and his frustration peaked. "Once you have details, let me know before you make any plans. I don't want to

argue about this, but we both have custody of Carly. Both of us. Remember that."

"I should have known." She hung up before he could finish.

He stood beside the phone, his body trembling. He knew Glenda well enough to sense she was making big plans for Carly. To agree to anything that wouldn't be good for his daughter was ridiculous. Never. He would fight Glenda if necessary.

"It's not a mansion, but it's a pretty nice place." Rick stood in the kitchen giving his sister the apartment tour. "I decided to take off work tomorrow."

"Tomorrow? Then I could have come on Thursday instead of today." Rene gave him a coy look he'd seen on his mother's face, as if her imagination meant more to her than what he said. "I was surprised when Mom hinted that something's going on with a woman."

"The woman is only a good friend." But he hadn't seen her since the kiss. Today at work he'd given in and gone to see her, but she'd left early for a dental appointment. Now he was left in limbo. "I've known her for about four years. We're coworkers."

Rene arched an eyebrow. "But I thought—"

"Company policy? Yes, although most of us think that's an outdated policy, but she and I are only friends…for now. But Angie is a woman I can see in my future, Rene. It's a long story. In fact, I have a list of things I'd like to talk to you about."

"Then let's talk. Tomorrow you might be with the family, and I don't think you want to talk then."

"You're right. How about the balcony?" He motioned toward it. "It's small, but I have a couple chairs out there, and the weather is gorgeous today."

She gave a nod and headed for the sliding door while he grabbed a couple of soft drinks from the refrigerator and followed her.

When they'd settled, he leaned back, not sure where to start. His mind swung from Glenda to Angie to Carly, and he tried to find a logical order in which to proceed. He failed. So much for logic. He'd start with what was most on his mind. "I made an appointment with my attorney to talk about issues I'm having with Glenda."

"What issues?" Her eyes narrowed as her brow furrowed. "I thought you two were working things out okay. It's been three years, Rick."

"It has, but it's never been smooth. We both wanted full physical custody and naturally I lost. Mothers usually win in court unless they're drug addicts or abusive and it can be proven. You know Glenda is a good woman. I wouldn't have asked her to marry me if she wasn't, but I didn't see the side of her that would cause problems."

"What's happening now to cause problems between you?"

He related the telephone call and his suspicions, and the more he relived it, the more his body responded to his frustration and anger. "She's not taking Carly to Europe, not even for a week."

An expression of concern came over Rene's face. "I understand why you're leery, but it would be a lovely experience for Carly. She's five going on six, isn't she? And Mom tells me she's bright as a star."

Though he managed a grin, he didn't feel it. In fact, he boiled inside. "She is, Rene, but think about it. Once Glenda has Carly out of the country, who knows what she could do. If she had already planned to keep her there, I would have a hard time getting her back. I can't take that chance. Glenda thinks of Glenda and what she wants."

He shook his head and dragged in a breath. "Even Carly sees that at times. I'm sorry that the child is so wise, but she truly has an understanding of her mom far beyond her years." He jerked his head upward. "And don't think I've coerced her or spoken badly of her mom. I haven't. I try to always speak with respect and—"

Rene flexed her palm to stop him. "Rick. You're my brother. I know you as well as anyone. You would never do that, so you don't need to defend your actions. I can see why you're afraid of what could happen. I understand why you're seeing your lawyer. It's a good idea."

His shoulders eased downward. "I'm glad you recognize my concerns. Sometimes I wonder if I'm the crazy one."

"Far from it, and remember, I know Glenda, too. The whole family saw her ways, and I think that's why you might have sensed Mom and Dad weren't the most joyful parents at the announcement of your engagement. But they knew you had brains and assumed you could handle it."

He averted his eyes, trying to sort out what she'd said. "I had no idea Mom and Dad weren't happy about the engagement. I know they didn't have much input into the wedding plans, but then, neither did I." The reality kicked him in the stomach. "I was stupid, it seems."

"No, you were blinded by love. I only wish she had the same devotion to you as you did to her. It's what keeps a marriage together. You don't think Hal and I would have made it all these years without that basic commitment. Love conquers all. Remember what scripture says? If you don't, read it. Corinthians 13 verses one to thirteen. It's one of the most beautiful explanations of love I've ever read."

"Okay, Mom."

Rene chuckled. "The older I get, the more of Mom comes out in me." She waved him on. "So, go ahead. What's the next problem?"

"It's not a problem, but Carly adores Angie, and that's caused competition with Glenda. Carly comes home from times with Angie bubbling about how much fun they have and what Angie is teaching her. I can't ask Carly not to say anything. I don't think she would understand."

"Whoa. That is an issue. Vindictiveness is a way to attack competition. We've seen evil things happen from envy." She shook her head, seeming lost in thought. "I suppose you don't want to stop spending time with her when Carly's with you."

"Rene, if you saw them together you'd better understand. Angie adores her. She's taught her so many things. Carly's learned to plant flowers. Angie let her select flowers for her beds at her home and taught her to set the table. I can't tell you the things that she's shown her, and Carly is proud as she learns these little things. I'm ashamed of myself for not realizing what she can learn. I'm learning from Angie, too."

"I'd like to meet her, Rick. She sounds amazing."

"She is."

"So what's stopping you from progressing? You said you're ignoring the company policy and I agree. It's antiquated."

"They have their reasons, but I'm hoping one day they'll see the error of it all. I don't think it's ever been challenged." His heart lifted. "Maybe Ang and I will be the first ones to do that."

Rene grinned. "Good for you, and she seems like the girl who could do that."

He glanced at his watch. "We'd better get going before we both starve. It's getting late, and the popular restaurants get crowded."

She rose and grabbed her handbag. "Let's go. I'm not one to stand in line for long."

He knew that. He slid open the balcony door and stepped

inside. "Thanks for listening, Rene. The person I love to talk with is Angie, and as you can see, some of our conversation makes it impossible."

"Gotcha."

Angie sat in the kitchen trying to feel her lips. She chuckled at the numbness that lingered following the small cavity filling. She'd suggested no local anesthetic, but her dentist had insisted on giving her the shot just in case. Anesthetic was worse than the filling.

Another thing as bad as the anesthetic was not seeing Rick. She'd been confused and had avoided him for a couple of days, and now she'd missed work. The gap seemed to widen since he hadn't called her. She gave up trying to eat dinner even though it was late. Eating once feeling had returned in her mouth made more sense.

She picked up her soft drink and headed outside. Though dusk lowered on the horizon, she breathed in the pleasant air. She lifted her shoulders and gazed at what she'd done to the flower beds. Her front beds were blossoming, and the wave petunias were spreading as the description had promised. She loved the colors Carly had selected. Obviously pink was her favorite color. Every blossom was a shade of pink from vivid to pastel.

She sank to the porch steps, her chest weighted with her reaction to Rick's kiss. She'd loved it. She'd been as much a part of it as he had. She needed to apologize. Yet admitting the truth seemed too much a commitment. Was she ready for it?

Hearing a sound, she rose and spotted a nice-looking middle-aged woman treading toward her with a scowl on her face. Angie had no idea what she'd done, but it had to be something. "Hello. You must be a neighbor I've never met."

"Birdie." She folded her arms across her ample chest. "I just came from having dinner in town with my cousin."

"How nice." Stymied as to why the visit, she waited.

"Nice for me, I suppose." She gazed at the yard. "Nice flowers. I saw that little girl helping you plant. Cheap labor."

Though a fleeting grin curved her mouth, her earlier demeanor returned. "And speaking of that little girl, is she yours?"

The abrupt question surprised her. "No, she's—"

"Your boyfriend's. If you think he's single, you have another think coming. He had dinner with his wife at the café where I just ate. If not his wife, then he has another woman. I noticed they were close, patting each other and laughing."

The blast of information spun her brain, and Angie fought to gather her wits. "Rick is a free man. We're not engaged. We're just good friends."

"Really?" She arched an eyebrow so high it nearly touched her hairline. "I thought you should know. Sorry to bother you, and I see that I've annoyed you from your expression. Some women want to know when they're being cheated on. I would. But apparently you're different."

A huff sounded in her voice as she turned and strode back up the street.

Angie watched her, finally able to close her gaping mouth, overwhelmed by utter disappointment. She'd trusted Rick's honesty and kindness. He'd finally broken her barriers of trust. Her relationship with Cal, all of his empty promises even with her attempts to please him, had ended in disgust. While in his company, she'd done things she'd known were wrong, but he'd hinted at marriage and a wonderful life. In her delusion she'd trusted him, and even before his accidental death she'd sensed she'd made a mistake. After his death,

she'd wallowed in disgust for behaving in a way that shamed her and had faced the fact that marriage never would have happened.

Then Rick had stepped into her life, but if Birdie was correct, her disillusionment would send her back in the past and she would never trust a man or her judgment again. The dinner she'd planned to eat later held no interest. She sank to the sofa and pressed her head against a decorative pillow, weighted with her thoughts.

When the phone rang, she jerked upward, dazed and nauseated, and then realized she'd fallen asleep. She searched for her cell phone and found it in the kitchen. By then the caller had hung up. She sank onto the nearest chair and searched through recent calls. Rick. Her heart lurched as a ragged breath ripped from her lungs.

Closing her eyes, she tried to make sense out of Birdie's visit and Rick's call. When she gazed at the phone again, she saw the blink of a voice message.

She tapped the icon that took her to the message center and keyed in the password, her heart in her throat. "Sorry, I missed you, Angie. I really wanted to talk with you in person. I tried today, but they said you'd taken off early to see the dentist. I had dinner with my sister tonight, and I made some plans. Could you call me when it's convenient? We haven't spoken in a couple of days, Ang, and I miss you."

Startled by his message and her accusation, moisture formed in her eyes. She dropped her head to the table, rocking her neck back and forth, as she tried to dislodge her shock at Birdie's accusation. She'd begun building defenses rather than admitting her feelings and trusting him. She'd only met Birdie and had been told about the woman's joy of sharing both truths and untruths. Rick meant the world to her. Why hadn't she asked him first? Losing him and Carly would be horrendous.

Managing to calm herself, Angie tossed her reaction aside and redialed Rick's number. When he answered, her heart stood still. "I didn't get to my cell phone on time. I couldn't remember where I'd left it."

"That's so unlike you, Ang. It seemed strange not seeing you or even talking with you. I guess we both took time to…"

He faltered and she understood why. "I'm going to be honest, Rick. I was angry at myself for enjoying your kiss. That sounds stupid, but I'm feeling overwhelmed. Our friendship has gone in directions I never expected and I—"

"And you're disappointed in me."

His tone broke her heart. "No, Rick. You did what I've wanted to do, but I couldn't admit it. You're an amazing man, and you mean so much to me. I'm afraid to act on it, and yet I plowed into the kiss with gusto."

"I know, and it took my breath away. I can't tell you how happy you made me."

"But I don't want to lead you on, Rick. If I were thinking commitment, you'd be the only man I would want to spend my life with. I'm comfortable with you and love your company. I love Carly with all my heart, and it's the first time in my life I can imagine what it would be like to have a child of my own. I don't want to let you go."

"Good, because I don't want to lose you, either. You mean too much to me. You're one of the only people I can talk with about things I need to get out of my system. I trust you. I admire you. I dream about you and what it would be like to spend my life with you."

His voice held a faint tremor that exposed his emotion, and her heart swelled. "I feel the same."

"Then let's stop fighting it, Angie. We have time. We're not going anywhere. Let's take it day by day. Any problems we come across will work out. If you need time, I'm

here. I can wait if I know that you feel the same. That's something I haven't known. Maybe I'm blind again, but—"

"Blind again?" Confused, she waited for his response.

"I had a talk with my sister, Rene, about Glenda's latest escapade."

He told her about his marriage and the new issue with taking Carly to Europe.

"Europe? I don't blame you for being concerned, Rick, and I'm glad you've made an appointment with your attorney. He'll give you the best guidance on that issue." Birdie's visit swept through her mind. "I needed your guidance earlier today, but I felt helpless and…it's a long story."

"I like long stories."

She waited a moment before admitting she'd fallen asleep crying. "Here's why I really missed your call, although it is true that I couldn't find my phone. I spent this afternoon crying myself to sleep. I haven't eaten since breakfast."

"Why? What happened?"

Birdie had happened. She related her neighbor's visit and the conversation. "Somehow I let her gossip make me believe that you'd ended our relationship and were out with an attractive woman."

"My sister is attractive. You'll see that when you meet her tomorrow."

"Tomorrow?"

"My mom's invited us to dinner. When school's out tomorrow, I'll pick up Carly, and when you're home, I'll come by, and we'll be on our way. By the way, let's not say anything about the attorney. I'll be talking with him tomorrow. I'd hate for Carly to overhear us."

"I understand." Her heart ached thinking of sweet little Carly being pulled into a parental tug-of-war. Yet Rick's fear was real. Once out of the country, he would have little control.

"On a nicer note, Mom's eager to meet you. I'm sure she's already planning the wedding."

"I guess we have the same problems with our moms."

He grinned. "By the way, Rene's anxious to meet you and Carly."

"I miss that child so much, Rick." Carly's image glowed in her mind. "And I miss you, too."

"Those are beautiful words, and to be honest, I figured I'd overstepped myself, and you were planning to end our friendship, so we were both being silly. It's a lesson learned. Good communication can end wrong deductions and it can resolve even the most serious problems. Let's promise to communicate. To talk when we're confused and worried. Can we promise?"

"I can, Rick. I hate what I felt. I love the way it is now." But as the words left her, she faced her own truth. She hadn't been totally honest with Rick about her past. If their relationship could grow, telling him the whole story was a must. But could she do it?

"Great. Open, honest and positive. I like that, and I promise, too."

He was silent a moment while she struggled with her obviously twisted promise.

"Ang, thanks. I'll see you after work tomorrow. And be prepared. This time you're the one on trial."

On Thursday, from the moment Angie and Rick walked into his mother's house, she hung on to her every word. The questions were more subtle than her mom's and Connie's, but the glint in Rick's eyes sent her a message. Revenge. Today was her turn for the shrewd grilling. Though Angie longed to refute Rick's grin, it was impossible with them all gaping at her. His mother's sweet smile and bright eyes helped her feel more at home. She'd noticed a photograph

of Rick's deceased father and she speculated what Rick might look like at his age. In the photo, gray was woven through his father's brown hair, yet he remained youthful looking, probably as good-looking as Rick would be when he was that age.

She had hoped that Carly would distract them, but no. Though they hugged her and doted on her, Carly didn't steal one bit of attention from Angie despite her hopefulness.

His mother's question bounced over her head, and Angie paused to think. "Yes, Rick and I have known each other quite a while. Four years plus. I noticed his sadness right after I started working there. It caught my attention. When he smiled, he was a light turned on in a dark room, but some days, the dark never brightened."

Mrs. Jameson lifted her shoulders as she eyed Carly's nearness. "That was a difficult time for him. For all of us because Ricky rarely said much to us. Still, we saw the same desolation."

Rick looked away, his focus on Carly playing across the room with her puzzles, but Angie sensed it was his way of avoiding the conversation. Finding himself discussed while he was sitting there couldn't be a pleasant experience.

Angie wished it hadn't happened, but in truth, Rick had talked with her about his troubles, and she'd never understood why he'd picked her. He had opened up to her more than once about his crumbling marriage and his worry about his little daughter. Strange, but in all those years, she'd never met Carly. Today his mother's admission caused her to feel guilty that he'd opened up to her. But she refused to think about it. At the time, Rick talking with someone had been important. She had just happened to be the person.

"You have a lovely home, Mrs. Jameson." Angie swept

her hand toward the far side of the room, hoping to redirect their conversation.

To her surprise, his mother grasped her hand on return. "Thank you. His dad and I loved our home, and now that he's gone, it's filled with all the memories. Ricky grew up in this house."

Ricky. Every time she heard his childhood nickname, Angie had to swallow her chuckle. She shifted her eyes to Rick's and watched a pink tinge grow on his cheeks. "I'm sure it was always a happy home."

Although she tried to ease her hand away, Mrs. Jameson strengthened the grip, her eyes focused on the ring finger of her left hand.

"Are you missing something here?" His mother sent Angie a grin before her gaze shifted to Rick's. "I thought—"

"Mom." Rick's tone had heightened. "Sometimes people like to enjoy their companionship without fanfare and invasion of privacy."

His mother's head flew back. "Invasion of what?" She shook her head. "I'm just asking if you two have any plans."

Angie opened her mouth to speak, but Rick's voice stomped across her effort. "Nothing specific at the moment. I'm sure you'll be the first…" He adjusted his gaze toward Angie's while she had to camouflage her reaction.

Rick smiled and turned back to his mother. "I'm sure, Mom, you'll be the second to know."

Mrs. Jameson took a moment to weigh his words and then grinned back. "Second will be fine, but don't dally. You're no longer a spring chicken, Ricky."

His head swung back with a laugh. "You'd never know." He faced Angie. "Whenever I hear 'Ricky,' I'm back in third grade."

"Can you remember that far back?" Angie jumped in,

adding some levity to the conversation. Anything to move it around to something else.

"Daddy can't remember far back, because he forgot to bring my new storybook to Grandma's, and I wanted to bring it." Carly had left her stack of puzzles and had gravitated into the conversation without anyone's awareness.

Angie was taken by surprise when Carly slipped to her side and settled next to her in the easy chair. Angie stroked Carly's hair. "Maybe that means he'll have to buy you another storybook."

"Does it, Daddy? I know the one I want."

Rick shook his head. "Two women against one man is unfair."

Everyone laughed, even Carly, who seemed to get the joke. But before the laughter had subsided, the child bent closer to Angie's ear. "Want to know what book I want?"

"I do. I always like to know your favorites."

Carly giggled. "Chocolate or strawberry when it's ice cream."

Angie tousled her hair. "But what about the book?"

"*Nancy Drew and the Clue Crew.* My friend at school told me about the story with clues and everything. Her mom helps her read it."

Angie's mind sailed to the past. "Want to know something?" Everyone was listening, but it was too late to stop now.

Carly's head bobbed.

"Nancy Drew was my favorite girl detective, and I read lots of stories about her when I was growing up."

"You did?" Carly's eyes widened. "Daddy, Angie—"

"I heard, sweetheart. I think Grandma even read them."

Rick's mom nodded. "I think I read the whole series."

Relief spread through Angie, seeing the conversation had finally shifted from her empty ring finger.

Mrs. Jameson rose. "Come with me, Carly, and I'll show you a bunch of my old reading books. I saved them for a day just like this."

Carly slipped off Angie's lap and skipped toward her grandmother.

"Mom." Rick stood a moment as he gave Angie the eye. "Angie and I are going out for a few minutes. I'll show her your garden."

"Great idea, Ricky. While you're gone, Carly and I will look at the books and then dish up dessert."

Relief swept across Rick's face. He reached for her hand and drew her toward the back of the kitchen and out the door.

When they stepped outside Angie stood a moment, appreciating the lovely yard but most of all the escape from the questions. She empathized with what she'd put Rick through at her parents' home.

"We escaped." He slipped his arm behind her back and drew her closer. "I'd hoped this wouldn't happen. I'm sorry I—"

Angie pressed her finger over his lips, a half grin on her face as she recalled his visit with her parents. "Don't apologize. Mothers want to know everything. To them we're still their child." She struggled to keep from smiling. "Isn't that right, Ricky?" She failed. Her laughter bubbled into the air. Her shoulders relaxed and Rick's tension faded, shown by the smile sneaking onto his lips.

"Thanks." He brushed her cheek with his free hand, a pink tinge on his face. "I forgot to warn you about—"

"And take away the fun. Nonsense." Reality marred the moment, and she shook her head. "I hope you came out here to tell me about the attorney. I've been longing to know what happened."

"I've wanted to tell you, but..." His shoulders drooped. "Carly is too smart for her knickers."

"Knickers?"

He shrugged. "You know what I mean. Nothing passes that child." He beckoned her forward away from the house. "Follow me to the flower beds. We're safer there."

They made their way through the mowed lawn to the lovely display of flowers across the back of the property. Sunlight spread across the earth and kissed the colorful blossoms. Kissed... Her mind flew back to the day that had made her life different. "What did he say?"

"From what he said, when both parents have legal joint custody and one parent wants to take the child out of the country, both parents must agree for the child to get a passport. It would take dire circumstances for the court to allow her to take Carly without my signature."

"Dire circumstances? Can you be sure she won't come up with something?"

"Glenda would need proof that the travel is for Carly's health needs or that something serious has happened in that country that Carly needs to be there. I don't think she can come up with that."

Her concern ebbed as she listened. "It sounds safe to me, Rick."

"She might use the 'mother's rights' tactic. She could say I'm depriving Carly from the amazing experience of visiting a foreign country."

"Would that make a difference?" Her concern veered back, causing another knot in her throat.

"I don't know. If I dally long enough she might not have time to fight me in court." His head lowered, his spirits deflated. "I don't put anything past Glenda."

"Then you'll have to fight for her. Press the point that

it's not a vacation but her mother must work. That might change the court's mind."

"But I work, too, Ang." He shook his head. "I started out being confident, and when I say it aloud, reality kicks me in the gut."

"Rick, what would Carly want? Does she have any rights? Do they listen to a child's preference?"

"Glenda could make the trip sound inviting. Carly's filled with curiosity. She might love the idea of traveling to a place that's different." His eyes moistened. "I've hoped she would want to stay here, but the more I think of it—"

"You doubt." She released a lengthy breath. "I understand, Rick. How about prayer? Maybe that's the answer."

His head popped up as if pulled by a rope. "Angie, thank you. Sometimes I forget to pray. Hard to believe, but my mind tangles in legalities and my need for keeping her with me, and…" He drew Angie to face him and wrapped his arms around her waist. "And you, Ang. You're the one who reminded me to pray. Thank you."

Her reminder surprised her, too. Somehow when she'd felt cornered, she'd recalled that humans had no power over their own destiny except through God's willingness to let them. She'd remembered that from years earlier. She'd heard God had a plan, but she also knew that God could revise His plan or His plan might be to let trouble appear to win and then make it go away.

Tension faded from Rick's face. "You. You amaze me, Angie, and I long to kiss—"

"Daddy!" Carly's voice split them apart. "What are you doing?"

Laughter bubbled from Angie's throat. "He was showing me the flowers, and—"

"Uh-uh." She slipped between them. "Daddy was looking at you, not the flowers."

Rick scooped her into his arms. "I was trying to decide which was prettier—flowers or Angie's eyes."

"Angie's prettier all over her." Carly giggled. "Grandma said it's time for dessert."

"I'm ready." Angie tweaked her nose. "And later you can tell me about Grandma's books, and maybe tomorrow or the next day, we can go to the bookstore and find that book you want."

"And we can bake cookies, too." She beamed.

Angie's heart melted.

Chapter Eight

Rick sat at Angie's kitchen table watching Carly learning to bake cookies. His chest constricted seeing the joy in his little girl's face and the same reflected in Angie's. She looked at life with a spirit he'd missed for so many years, and she possessed a deep love for children. Although she rarely talked about her sister's children, he understood now, learning the two tended to be rude and undisciplined. Spoiled children were difficult to admire. He thanked the Lord for the gift of Carly's sweet nature.

He couldn't keep his eyes off Angie's patient teaching. She lit up the room, and she lit up Carly's world, too. As soon as Carly knew Angie would be spending time with them, her expression had changed to delight. A little smile permeated her face and wouldn't fade unless a serious situation broke the spell. In truth, he would never find another woman who gave him and his daughter that kind of joy. But nothing was certain. His longing could end up only a dream and nothing else.

His happiness faded, and he allowed his mind to drag him down. Since he'd talked with Glenda, he'd worried that she would get what she wanted. The thought of her taking Carly to Europe sapped his energy and his joy. Though his

attorney assured him he had to sign for the passport, he pictured Glenda manipulating some way to get what she wanted. And if she did, had she been honest with him? Was the trip for only a week or two? Since he'd talked it over with Angie when they'd escaped into his mom's backyard, his what-ifs hadn't given him peace.

But peace was what he needed. Pulling his mind to the present, he refocused on the baking lesson and burst into laughter. "Are you two having a flour fight?" He shook his head. Angie had encouraged Carly to measure the flour into a two-cup container. Instead, with her unsteady hands, she'd sprinkled a couple more cups across the counter and onto the floor. "Carly, my girl, you've made a mess."

"Daddy!" Although she'd tried to grin, he realized he'd hurt her feelings.

Angie noticed Carly's expression too and, as always, tried to save the day. "Look what we did, Carly." She gave her a hug. "I've done this, too. Flour has a mind of its own."

"Flour doesn't have a mind, does it?" Carly tilted her head, a thoughtful look on her face.

"No." She tweaked his daughter's cheek. "I was teasing." She eyed the semi-disaster and gave him a head toss. "The broom is in the hall closet. Will you get it for us?"

He rose but couldn't contain himself. "Where are you going?"

"Going?" She squinted at him. "I…" Her confusion turned to understanding. "Rick, I'm not going anywhere on a broom."

Carly slammed her floured fists onto her apron-covered sides. "Daddy. Angie is not a witch. She's a beautiful princess." She gave Angie's waist a hug, the flour tracing her handprint.

He winked at her. "I know. Guess what I was doing?"

After studying him a second, she lowered her fists.

"You were teasing, but Daddy, you always tell me not to be mean, and that was mean."

His face drooped from a grin to one of guilty admission. "It was. Should I sit in the corner or wash my mouth out with soap?"

She shook her finger at him. "Just don't do it again." She tittered. "But you can get the broom."

He nodded, proud that she remembered what he'd taught her even though Angie's half grin let him know she was enjoying Carly's reprimand. He strode to the hallway, located the broom and swept the flour into a dustpan. "I did my penance."

"What's pennas?"

Angie grinned. "*Penance* means he finished his punishment. What do you think? Should we forgive him?"

Carly smiled at him. "I forgive you, Daddy."

He thanked her and sank back into the chair, watching her refocus on the cookies. Angie had the dough mixed, and they began forming the cookies. Carly rolled the dough into balls and put them on a cookie sheet while Angie flattened the tops with a fork, making a crisscross pattern. Before long the scent of peanut butter cookies filled the air.

After the last batch had been baked and cooled, Angie gave them each a cookie and then took a large plastic container and one smaller and stacked the treats inside. "It's too early for dinner, so let's walk down the street. I'll introduce you to El, and Carly can give him the cookies. He loves them."

"So do I."

Angie rolled her eyes at him.

"Who's El?" Carly gave Angie a curious look.

"His real name is Elwood Barnes and he's my very nice neighbor. You'll like him."

"Okay." She slipped from the stool and waited for Angie to let her carry the small container.

Rick enjoyed watching them interact. Angie treated Carly like a grown-up, with more patience than he had. She gave Carly the box, and she skipped toward the front door while they followed.

Outside the sun gilded the landscape, and warmth aroused the aroma of the lilacs. As he neared Angie, he sensed she too emitted the same scent from somewhere on her person. Carly bounded ahead of them, her head shifting from side to side as if taking in all she could see. When she came to a stop and spun around, he shifted his gaze to what must have interested her.

Ahead he spotted a little girl playing in a front yard across the street a few houses down. He motioned to Angie, but she only shrugged. "Have you seen the child before?"

"No. They moved in a week or so ago, and I really didn't notice much of anything, but if you want details we can check with Birdie."

He chuckled. "She's the bearer of news."

"That's a nice way to say she's the local gossip."

Carly had turned back to the girl, and when he reached her, she looked at him, her eyes bright with interest. "Who are they?"

Angie put her arm around Carly's shoulders. "I don't know, but we'll find out soon enough." She motioned to the next house. "This is where El lives, and they're right across the street. He'll know."

Angie led the way up the walk, and before she climbed the porch steps, an elderly gentleman pushed open the door with a smile, his eyes twinkling. "Angie, what a nice surprise, and you brought company."

He stepped onto the porch and down the steps, his hand extended. "I'm Elwood Barnes, and you must be Rick."

"Guilty as charged." He clasped the man's palm, surprised at his strong grip. "Angie's spoken well of you, Mr. Barnes."

He waved the words away. "El. Call me El." He shifted his gaze downward. "And this must be Carly. I've heard only good things about you, missy."

She smiled, her eyes beaming. "You're a nice man, too. Angie said so."

"Well, my word, Angie's my best neighbor."

Angie made a subtle motion toward the cookies.

Carly caught on and extended the container. "We made you peanut butter cookies today."

"For me?" His merry chuckle brightened the air. "You know how to make an old man happy."

She nodded and inched closer. "Do you know that girl?" She pointed across the street.

"Not very well, but she seems like a good girl. She moved in last week with her uncle."

"Where's her mommy?" Carly gazed across the street, watching her every move.

"Her mommy is ill, I think. Very sad."

"She's sick?" She studied El for a moment. "And so the girl can't be with her mom?"

"Her mom's out of town." El shot Rick a look of regret as if he realized he'd stepped into a hornet's nest. "I didn't think—"

Rick shook his head. "I'm sure the little girl is in really good hands with her uncle."

El jumped in. "Yes, he spends a lot of time with her."

"I spend time with my daddy, and we have lots of fun with Angie. She's my favorite friend." She smiled, followed by a titter. "I mean a grown-up friend."

Angie chuckled and wrapped her arm around Carly.

"And you're my favorite almost six-year-old friend in the whole world."

"I am?" Carly hugged her back.

Rick's heart lurched watching Carly's unrestrained affection for Angie. Glenda's ability to show affection had been thwarted by something. She'd always been that way, but Glenda was pleasant and hardworking. Yet he'd fallen for her, and as their marriage had deteriorated, he'd tried to fix it but couldn't. Now he understood. Glenda needed validation. Despite her appearance of confidence, somewhere inside she doubted herself. Her vulnerability had captured his "Rick to the rescue" gene, and his feelings for her covered the flaws he'd hoped would change with time.

The experience taught him a life lesson. A person's flaws rarely changed unless the person made the effort to change them. His efforts didn't make one iota of difference. He'd taught Carly to express joy and love, and she did. It seemed to be natural. Glenda didn't have the impetus. Nothing he did made an impact. He'd learned that change could happen only as a gift from Glenda and only if she wanted it that way. The struggle saddened him.

But Angie, she was a natural just as Carly was. Her affection showed in everything she did, and for that reason his affection had grown, maybe too much. Though he and Angie had opened up a little with her feelings, sometimes her restraint reminded him that nothing between them was a sure thing.

A buzz vibrated against his leg just before the faint ringtone sounded in his pocket. He made a half turn and slipped out his cell phone. Glenda. On his cell? Tension knotted his shoulders, anticipating what she wanted. "Excuse me a minute." He managed a pleasant look and displayed his cell phone. "Business."

El and Angie nodded, but Angie's face revealed her curiosity.

He stepped away from the discussion that had shifted to neighborhood events and Rema's plight. Carly's attention seemed glued to the child across the street.

When he had distanced himself, he answered. "Glenda?"

"Let me get right to it, Rick. I've run into a snag. My plans have broadened and I'll be staying a bit longer in Europe, which means—"

"What does 'a bit longer' mean, Glenda?" He clamped his jaw, fearing his thoughts would break free.

"At least a month. The job is bigger than I expected. Naturally I'll find a tutor for—"

"But you won't need a tutor. You have a big job to deal with, and I'll love having more time with Carly. Your job is important to you. Why not focus—"

"Are you insinuating that Carly isn't important to me?" Her pitch rose along with her volume.

"I'm not insinuating anything. I'm speaking reality. You'll be in Germany to accomplish your company's work. That's the reason you're going. Finding child care for Carly means she'll be away from both of us in a place where everyone is a stranger. It doesn't make sense."

"Rick, it will broaden her. Do you want to thwart her chance to grow and learn—"

"She's five years old, Glenda. Five. She'll have many years to learn and broaden her knowledge of the world. Yes, I want her to experience new things, but… Listen, I'm with some friends, and this isn't a good time to discuss this. Let me call you back once I'm alone."

"Are you evading me? The answer is easy. I need you to approve her passport. Sign it and that's all you have to do, Rick. Write your name on the form."

"But that's approving the trip, Glenda. I don't approve of that."

"I'd hoped it wouldn't come to this, Rick, but if you want to play games, I can get out the big guns. I'll be talking with my attorney."

"That's up to you. I've already spoken with mine and Friend of the Court. You need my approval, and you're not going to get it. I'm going to hang up now and talk with you later. Or maybe our attorneys will talk. Whichever you prefer."

During her silence, he clicked off the call and turned off the volume button and put it on vibrate. He had no intention of arguing now while he was with Carly and…

He closed his eyes, willing his frustration to die, and when he looked up, El and Angie were still talking while Carly's interest remained with the girl and their subtle glances aimed toward each other.

As he strode back to them, he glanced at the other side of the street and spotted the child's uncle at the front door. He pushed it open and stepped to the porch. His daughter bounded to him, her voice pealing through the air but her words unclear.

El gave the man a wave, and the man gestured back before turning his attention to the child.

Rick ambled toward Angie, watching questions flicker in her eyes. He lifted a shoulder to let her know something had happened, but she was wise enough not to ask.

Rick managed to contain his grin when he realized El didn't give up easily. El raised his hand again and finally got the uncle's attention. He beckoned the man to join them. After a slight hesitation, the uncle and his young niece followed.

When the family neared, El motioned toward Angie. "I thought you'd like to meet one of our nicest neighbors,

Angie Bursten, and her friend Rick and his daughter, Carly." He rested his hand on the man's shoulder. "Angie, this is Doug Billings and his niece."

Rick grasped Doug's hand while the girls eyed each other. "Nice to meet you, Doug." He grinned at the little girl. "And who do we have here?"

Doug released an uncomfortable chuckle. "My niece, Kimmy. Kimmy's six, but she'll notify you that she'll be seven in a few months."

Carly couldn't let that issue drop. "I'm almost six."

Rick hid his chuckle, noting Carly's pride in being almost the same age as Kimmy.

Carly finally shifted her gaze to Kimmy. "Do you like to play?"

Kimmy shrugged. "I play at school and sometimes when Uncle Doug has time."

Kimmy eyed Carly. "Do you live in that house with the pretty flowers?"

Carly nodded, but faltered as El's voice cut through her response.

"One of the prettiest houses on the block, I'd say."

"Thank you, El." Angie gave him a grin and motioned to Carly. "Kimmy asked you a question."

Carly lowered her head. "No, but I wish I did." She paused as if to check Angie's expression. "I helped plant the flowers."

Rick's chest tightened. His apartment wasn't the best for Carly and he'd always felt bad about that. He had hoped to make a solid down payment soon and buy a home they could be proud of. Divorce, and all that went with it, had cut into his finances, yet he didn't want to cheat Carly out of a good life. "One day we'll have a house like Angie's." He gave Carly a telling look. "But it's nice Angie invites us here."

Carly gave a fervent nod. "I love Angie's house, but best, I love Angie."

Angie's face colored, and her eyes sought Rick's as mist grew along the brim of her lashes. "I've never heard anything as lovely, Carly." She slipped her arm around her and gave her a squeeze.

A smile lit Carly's face as she leaned closer and whispered a request. Angie gave her a wink.

Carly's spirit returned as she eyed Kimmy. "Do you want to come to Angie's and play?"

The girl gave Doug a plaintive look. "Can I, Uncle Doug?"

"Why don't you all come down?" Angie spread her arms wide. "We haven't eaten yet. How about if I order pizza?"

"Pizza!" The response from the two children pelted the air.

Rick shook his head. "That sounds like a rousing acceptance." He eyed Doug. "What do you say, and you too, El? This is a good time to get to know our neighbors." Though Doug's acceptance sounded strained, he agreed to join them and hurried to follow Kimmy already on her way.

El gave Rick a wink. "Thank you, but I already have dinner thawing. Maybe another time."

"Okay this time, but I'll remember that." Rick extended his hand, managing a smile though his mind was heavy with his recent conversation with Glenda. "And by the way, El, it was nice of you to introduce us to the new family. Doug will benefit from making new friends, and the little girl can use a distraction." He paused, not knowing how to say what was on his mind. "Angie told me you're a man who has the right things to say and one to talk with in a crisis."

El chuckled. "Now, that's a lot of credit to give an old

guy like me. My source of wisdom is free to everyone. It's all in the Good Book, where all wisdom comes from."

Rick squeezed his hand. "Thank you, El. I need to remember that. I'm always searching for answers to problems and forgetting to share them with the Lord. I'm facing a big one right now." He stopped himself. If he had the time, he'd spill out his story and listen to El's kind voice remind him of what scripture said. "But I have a daughter up ahead, so you get a reprieve."

El grasped his shoulder. "Anytime, young man. I'm here if you need me. Anytime."

"Thank you." He gave El a pat. "And that's from my heart." With a wave, he managed to move down the sidewalk to join the others. He trudged forward as if his legs were restricted by weights.

As she neared the house, Angie glanced behind her, wondering what had kept Rick. Something had happened. The business call didn't really make sense. And then she had thought about Glenda. Her business seemed to be driving Rick's life into the pits. He deserved so much more. Each day she viewed him with new eyes. Any woman would love to meet a man like Rick, and here she had known him for years and had never seen him in that light until recently. Now she couldn't see him without admitting Rick was what women called a keeper. She cringed, fearing the call wasn't good news, and surrounded by company meant waiting until later to learn what had happened.

After she climbed the porch steps, she pulled open the screen and waved them in.

They traipsed into the living room, while Rick headed for the phone to order the pizza. Carly whispered to Kimmy and then swung around. "Do you have a ball that we can play with outside? Not a little one but a bigger one?"

"A ball? A bigger ball?" Her mind shifted to what she might own.

Carly clapped her hands and cheered. "We can play tag with it." She gave a little shrug. "Or maybe—"

"Kick the ball or dodge the ball." Carly's creativity tickled her and triggered memories from her childhood. "I can show you how to play if I can find a ball."

"What's all the cheering?" Rick slipped into the room, and though he wore a pleasant grin, Angie's heart tugged seeing tension in his stance.

"We're going to play ball." Carly's face beamed.

Angie's mind whirred. "I'll have to look for one." She turned to Rick, longing to be with him. Not only did she want to know about the call, but she missed their time alone together. "Rick, do you want to help? You're better at digging through my storage cartons." Images of Rick spilled through her—toting boxes, hanging pictures, locating things she couldn't find in her moving boxes. It had been the day they'd grown closer. The day that had made a major change in her life.

"I will as soon as I order the pizzas, Ang." He tilted his head and grinned.

A chorus of pizza choices rang to the ceiling as the girls bounced around eager to name their preference while Angie added two antipasto salads.

Rick chuckled and jotted down the orders.

Angie clapped her hands. "Okay, everyone outside while we search for a ball." She gave Rick a knowing look and steered Doug and the girls through the back door. Her pride rose looking at the colorful flower beds that she and Carly had created. They added to the warm sunshine and joyful spirit she admired in the girls.

She crossed the yard, opened the garage door and stepped into the shadowed space.

Doug had followed her inside while the girls remained outside, creating what seemed to be a version of tag. "Can I help, Angie?"

"You sure can." She studied him, noting that his uneasiness detracted from his good looks. "I'm sorry about this mess. I forgot about it, or maybe *ignored* is a better word." She grinned and motioned to a stack of boxes. "If you want to tackle those, I'll look in this pile."

She heard him tear open a lid as she shifted boxes and read the labels. "How long has your sister been ill, Doug?"

The silence deepened, and finally she heard his sigh.

"About a month and a half."

She shook her head and faced him. "That's not easy for Kimmy or you."

He lowered his head with a shake. "Kimmy gets the brunt. I was ill-equipped, never having kids of my own."

She thought of Rick and his frustration with sharing Carly. The back and forth from one parent added confusion to a child's life, but it was a problem that wasn't easy to resolve. Her shoulders knotted with the situation, yet her heart rose when she knew Carly would be with them. *Them?* The word resounded in her ears.

"Don't blame yourself, Doug. No one anticipates serious problems like this. We all want a rosy future. It's part of who we are." Though Carly and Rick remained vivid, her thoughts swept back to Cal and the promising future she'd envisioned with him. Her world had come crashing down and bearing with it the bad mistakes she'd made. "But Kimmy seems to be holding up. She looks happy."

"She misses her mom, but she rises above it better than I do at times." He lifted his head. "You'd think I'd deal with it, knowing it's temporary, but Roseanne is my only sibling."

Life had unpleasantness along with the joys. She'd

learned that in her own life, but moving on was an important step to healing. Why couldn't she cling to that thought? Rick was there and a joy in her life. She had no advantage hanging on to the negatives.

"Don't be sorry, Doug. It's natural to care about family." A mental slap reminded her of her situation with Connie.

Doug returned to searching the boxes and she did the same. The search struck a chord about her new life. She'd never thought about having things around for children. She should have a few outdoor toys for them, but that hadn't entered her mind. Her niece and nephew always brought toys with them.

Hearing Carly's giggle sailing through the open door caused her heart to hitch. Times had changed since she'd met Carly. She grinned at the child's sweet voice. "Any luck, Doug?"

"Not yet, but you have a nice collection of potting soil and indoor fertilizer."

She chuckled as Rick appeared at the door. "Progress?"

"Not yet." She gave him a desperate look. "I'm still reading labels on the boxes."

Rick strode toward her. "Pizza and salad in a half hour, so let's find that ball." He broke the tape on the carton nearest him without reading the label and dug into the contents. He pulled out a few small tools, hammer, screwdriver, pliers and tape measure. Pretty feeble but they were tools she usually kept in the house. Her chest tightened as she recalled Rick using a few tools to hang the wall decor. Watching him, her heart flipped in her chest as she thought of so much that had happened since then. It seemed years ago and not just weeks.

"Beach ball." Rick's voice broke into her thoughts.

"That's it."

He chuckled. "Ang, that's pretty pathetic, but we'll live with it."

She managed a grin. He was right. She needed toys for kids, and she would get them.

Doug moved to Rick's side. "It'll work. One thing I've learned—a kid can make anything into a toy."

While the men blew up the ball, she hurried inside to gather plates, silverware and juice boxes for the kids. She'd begun to purchase treats for Carly since she'd become a wonderful fixture in her life, the same as Rick.

With his name in her mind, Rick came through the door. "Ball is ready and Doug's tossing it while the girls have to dodge getting hit. They love the game."

Though she wanted alone time, she pointed to the tray. "I'm fine if you want to join them."

He tapped his watch. "The pizza will be here and I'm waiting to pay." He touched her arm and drew her around. "And I wanted to tell you about the call."

Her heart lurched. "Bad news, I'm afraid."

He nodded. "Glenda's finally admitted the trip is for a month, but I still think she's covering the truth. I'm guessing it's even longer. She can't obtain Carly's passport without my signature, which—"

"You've refused to sign." Her throat constricted, imagining the worst.

"Absolutely, but she's threatening me with her attorney." He clasped her more tightly. "When it comes to Carly, Ang, I don't threaten easily. I've already talked with my attorney since I fear Glenda won't give up. I'm so afraid of where this is going to lead."

Emotion filled his voice while she trembled. "A court battle could involve Carly."

He nodded, tears brightening his eyes. "That's the last thing in the world I want. You know that, but I can't back

down on this, Ang. I can't…even though I know judges can be biased."

"Rick, I'm so sorry. I'm speechless. Every thought that enters my mind is useless. Nothing makes sense."

He rested his head on hers, releasing the pent-up emotion he'd hidden until then. Instead of speaking empty words, she held him close, her own body taut with her concern. What would happen? How would Carly be affected if it became a legal battle? Yet Rick couldn't bear to have Carly gone that long.

Neither could she. The vision filled her mind. No longer would life be the same without the joy of a child. Marriage. Children. They'd held no attraction, but now? Her heartbeat raced as she imagined life without the delightful child she'd grown to love. Reality swelled inside her. She wanted a daughter, specifically Carly. No going back could happen now. The words had been spoken. She loved Carly…the amazing daughter of her heart.

Chapter Nine

Rick hung up the phone for a second time. The first call had been to Glenda. He'd suggested they get together to talk, but she wanted no part of it. Her pitchy voice had split his ears. "I don't want to look at your selfish face, Rick."

Her words dug deep. He'd asked himself if Glenda was right and tried to put himself in her shoes, but he faced facts. If he had to travel for a month in a foreign country on business, he would never insist on taking Carly with him. Dragging her off and then dumping her on a caregiver as if she didn't matter would have broken his heart. Yes, they had to do it now for a couple of hours, but then they came home and picked her up from the day care. In Michigan, Carly didn't face a language barrier. She didn't have to deal with—

He stopped himself. Being in Germany would give her a chance to learn a new language. Carly was smart. Children learned fast. Could he hold her back from the wonderful experience?

The question died even as it rose. His head said one thing, but his heart spoke the truth. He couldn't do it. He'd lose his daughter. Glenda had something in mind, something she hadn't told him. He knew her well enough to spot

her manner of maneuvering situations. She ended up making him the guilty person. He'd experienced it over and over. But not this time. He'd stick to what his heart said.

At the end of that call, he'd contacted his caseworker from Friend of the Court. Having a woman assigned to his case had given him a bad vibe, but he'd found her able to listen and weigh decisions fairly. Today she'd listened and suggested getting together with Glenda and him to talk it over. Rick prayed the woman really understood his concern. Next he had to wait and see if Glenda would meet with the caseworker and him.

Carly ambled into the room, looking lost. "Aren't we going to Angie's?"

"I'm giving her a break."

A quizzical expression crept across her face. "A break from us?"

He managed to grin. "We'll see her later, okay?"

She sank onto the sofa. "I guess I'll have to wait." She folded her arms across her chest with a forlorn expression that made him chuckle. He hurried to her and scooped her into his arms. Carly wiggled as she laughed.

The house phone rang, breaking the fun, and he had to set her down. "You wait there." He slipped into the kitchen for the wall phone. Before he answered he spotted Glenda's phone number on the caller ID. He closed his eyes and picked up the receiver.

Before he could speak she began her tirade. "I can't believe you want to waste my time with that caseworker. Who is she? No one that matters since I've already talked to my attorney. He thinks you're selfish and ridiculous. So do I. If you don't cooperate in four days, I'll have to see you in court. Time's running out, Rick."

"Glenda, do you really want to do that? Do you want Carly dragged into this? We can't do that to her."

A sarcastic laugh flew across the line. "If you really care about your daughter being dragged into court, then sign the forms." She hung up.

His heart in his throat, he lowered the receiver and stood a moment to get his bearings. The situation made him sick. She'd done what he feared and placed the blame on him. His breathing grew labored, like an engine chugging up a hill. He closed his eyes. *Lord, I need help.*

Angie's face glowed in his mind. He needed to talk, but with Carly it was always difficult.

Gathering his wits, he managed a neutral expression and strode back into the living room. Carly still lay on the floor, but she'd devised some kind of game that seemed to involve exercises. "I saw this on TV, Daddy. See." She rolled onto her belly and attempted a push-up. After a moment she got the hang of it and pushed herself from the floor for an instant before sinking back down. "I'm bored."

"What about all your puzzles and—"

"I left them at Angie's." She gave him a melt-his-heart look. "Can we go there now?" When he didn't respond, she rose and wrapped her arms around him. "Please."

He wouldn't be good company with so much on his mind, but he agreed to call and see if they could come. She clung to him as he hit the number and waited. Finally he heard Angie's hello.

Her tone gave him concern. "Did I interrupt something?"

"No, not really. I hadn't given thought to dinner, and now I'll have to go out and pick up some groceries."

His mind snapped. "Here's a thought. I'd like to run an errand without Carly. Why don't you two go out to dinner on me? You'd be doing me a favor and how about letting

me know where. Maybe I can join you. If not, I'll see you back at your house. Will that work?"

"Sure, Rick."

Her response didn't sound totally convincing.

"But what's up?"

He'd feared she'd ask, with Carly hanging on to every word. "Carly's anxious to see you, so we can talk about it later, okay?"

Her faint chuckle warmed him. "I get it. That's fine. I'll see you shortly, and it works out well for me. I want to buy a few things for kids to play with when they're here, and Carly can help me pick out some things."

"Ang, you don't have to do—"

"Have to has nothing to do with it. I want to. See you shortly."

No point in trying to convince her otherwise. He said goodbye and gave Carly a nod. "Okay, get ready. You and Angie are going shopping and I think out to dinner."

She bounded from his lap and skipped out of the kitchen without a sound except for her giggles.

What a woman. Angie rolled with every request. She didn't insist it go her way. He found her refreshing, and now he hoped that El had a few minutes to talk. He longed to gain the man's wise counsel, but before he arrived there, he wanted to pray.

Carly shot into the living room before he could think. "Ready. Let's go."

He slipped his arm around her shoulders, and they walked out the front door and headed to his car. Carly prattled on about dinner and shopping and seeing Kimmy, leaving him no time to talk with the Lord. Without a minute of silence, he pulled in front of Angie's house, leaving her driveway free, and parked. Carly snapped off her seat belt and was out of the booster seat in a shot.

Angie stood in the front door and opened her arms as Carly darted up the porch steps. When Angie stepped out, she wrapped Carly in her arms. "I missed you."

"I missed you, too." Her smile wrenched through his chest. The weight of his mess with Glenda had nearly laid him low, but the horrible moment hit him with another warning. What would he and Carly do if she said goodbye? What would she do? Wither and die? The thought came without warning as distress drained his energy. "Lord, I do need help."

Rick slipped from the car and made his way up the sidewalk, forcing a bounce into his step and a smile that made his cheeks ache.

Angie's look said what he feared. She didn't believe the smile. The woman was uncanny.

She touched his hand. "Talk later, okay?"

He could only nod. "Have fun, and I may join you sooner than expected. I'm hoping to talk with El. The man has a special knack, and I want to bounce my thoughts off someone."

She nodded. "I understand, and I approve. Unbiased and wise."

"When he didn't join us for pizza the other day, I told him I owed him. Maybe I'll take him out tonight." He studied her expression.

She tilted her head and kissed his cheek. "We'll go to Greg and Lou's. You know where that is?"

"I do. I'll call you if I'm coming. If not, I'll see you when we're done." He wanted to kiss her. It seemed forever but Carly was too close and he feared she wouldn't understand.

He waited while she locked the house and he waved to them as they pulled down the street. Then he drew up his shoulders and headed down the block.

* * *

Angie leaned back, pleased that she'd stumbled on Greg and Lou's Restaurant. Though a down-home style establishment with wallpaper and lacy curtains filled with booths and tables, she loved their home-cooked fare and the fast and friendly service. She watched Carly finish the last of her spaghetti from their children's menu, winding the pasta around her fork. It made her grin. Simple pleasures that only children would appreciate. If only she could find as much fun in the simple things.

Her dinner special, chicken fettuccine with Alfredo sauce, had been excellent, with a creamy sauce and tasty pieces of poultry, but she faltered, recalling that Carly had her eye on their strawberry shortcake. The dessert appeared to be ice cream between two round cakes covered in berries and topped with a pile of whipped cream.

The memory took her back to her days as a child and looking forward to her mom's treats. If Carly became her stepdaughter, she would find delight in preparing surprises for her and teaching her more about cooking so she would become a loving mother, too. Mother? An image rose again of tucking her in bed and kissing her good-night. Though she loved the idea, the possibility seemed unreal, too wonderful to come true. "Ready for dessert, or are you too full?" She studied Carly's expression and had to bite her lip to keep from laughing. Carly's expression made it clear she was full but she was not one to give up a treat.

"I have a little room. Can we share?"

She winked. "Sharing is fun, and we'll get on with our shopping."

"To buy yard toys?" Carly's eyes twinkled.

"I think we need a couple of things, don't you?"

Carly tittered as a smile filled her face. "I'm lucky, Angie, 'cause I have two homes."

"You do."

She lowered her eyes a moment, then lifted them as if she had something she wanted to say but was afraid to.

"What's wrong, sweetheart?"

"Can I tell you a secret? A real secret?" Her comment came out in halted spurts.

A secret. The word caught in her throat. How could she keep something from Rick if it were something serious? But Carly needed someone. She drew in a breath. "What about your daddy?"

She lifted one shoulder. "I feel bad telling."

"Okay. I'll keep your secret…unless it's something that might hurt you or—"

"This won't hurt me." A faint grin flickered on her face.

"Tell me. I'll keep your secret."

Carly looked relieved. "I have two homes, but…I like my daddy's the best. I can't tell my mother because she would be sad."

Angie's heart flinched. She understood Carly's predicament. Rick would be thrilled but her mother certainly wouldn't, and with Carly's comment, her concern rose. She longed to know if Carly knew of her mother's trip and her plan to take Carly along. Still, she couldn't ask, even though it broke her heart. "You don't have to tell your mom, Carly. Your dad would be happy to hear you say that, but if you don't feel comfortable telling him then it can be our secret."

She nodded, a look of relief spreading across her face. "I really love to come to my dad's now 'cause you're with us, and you're fun and like to be with me."

"Your daddy loves to be with you."

"I know, and my mom does, but she always has to work too much. Even when she's home she wants me to be quiet so she can work."

A sigh escaped her as she listened to the five-year-old

bearing the weight of the world. "Adults have to work. That's hard on families sometimes, Carly. I know you wish she could spend more time with you."

She gave a big nod. "Daddy works, but he always spends time with me."

Angie didn't have an answer, and rather than making a placating comment, she didn't respond.

With no mention of the upcoming trip, she decided to let it go, and when the waitress arrived, they dug into the delicious strawberry shortcake. With a full belly, she paid the bill and they headed for the supercenter to look for outdoor games.

Carly jiggled in the back like a jumping jack tied to her chair, and Angie finally couldn't hold back her laughter. "You had too much sugar."

"No, I'm just happy to go shopping and look for toys."

"We're almost there." And it had to be soon before she kicked a hole in the back of the passenger seat. Angie grinned at seeing Carly in a confined situation.

After Angie arrived, she and Carly slipped from the car and made their way into the store and down the aisles until they spotted the games and toys.

"Let's get a ball." Carly bounded along the aisle, passing the boccie ball sets.

"Carly, look at these."

She studied the eight colorful balls. "I think we need a bigger ball than those."

Angie grinned. "This is a game." She explained the game and put the boccie set into her basket.

After she'd selected a ring-toss game and the bigger ball, Carly was satisfied. Angie's dreams became more vivid. She pictured what it would be like to have Carly in her life always. The child brought her joy just as Rick had done. She could no more dislodge the image than she could walk away

from Rick and Carly. They both had become her world. Her dilemma grew stronger, and she knew the past had to be brought into the open. Rick's faith had taught her that in the Lord there was hope, and that was what she needed to trust.

As they headed toward the checkout, Carly's questioning look roused her from her thoughts. Before she could divert her curiosity, Carly stopped beside a display of luggage. "Did Daddy tell you my mom's going on another trip?"

She slowed to a halt, her heart in her throat as she decided how to answer. She settled on the truth. "He did. Your mom's going to Germany, I think."

"For weeks." She gave Angie a plaintive look. "That's too long."

Struggling for a noncommittal response, she realized what she had to say. "You'll miss her, but the time will pass fast."

"I can't miss her."

Angie tried to stop her jaw from sagging. "You can't?"

"She wants me to go with her." A troubled look washed over her face. "I don't know—"

Angie couldn't make her mouth move. She stared at the child, heart in her throat knowing she had to say something, but not having the words to speak. Instead she knelt at her side and took her in her arms. "We'll see, sweetheart." She rubbed her back and held her tight, hoping that her action would help the child know that she was loved. After a few strange looks from customers, she eased up and scooted Carly in front of her. "Help me push the basket. Your daddy is waiting for us to get back."

Carly smiled at her, and she had all she could do to keep from sobbing.

Rick pushed the plate holding the rest of his chicken stew aside and leaned back while he listened to El shar-

ing stories of the good old days and especially of his wife. Rick longed to be blessed with a marriage filled with the kind of love El and his wife seemed to have shared. Somehow they'd segued from his own tale of woe about Glenda's plans for Carly in Europe to marriage in general. He hated to reintroduce his problem, but that was why he'd come.

El cleaned up the last of his goulash with a thick piece of bread and then rested his back on the bench and grinned. "I haven't forgotten about your problem, Rick. I'm thinking about what Jesus would do in your situation. My conclusion is this. Our job is to raise our children with common sense and with love. But that still doesn't answer your question, does it?"

Before Rick could speak, El continued, his eyes twinkling. "So let me give you some things to think about. There's a verse somewhere, I think in Deuteronomy, that says you should teach your children and talk to them in your house, and when you walk together and when you lie down, and when you rise. Now, I know we are to teach them about the Lord, but I think God wants us to teach more than scripture. We can teach them about life, too." He frowned and then turned to Rick. "What do you say?"

"In full agreement, El."

"But did you hear what the scripture says? 'And talk to them in your house.'" He tilted his head. "Did you talk to Carly about this problem? See what she wants and then weigh it against what common sense tells us. Ask yourself what is the best for her."

"I haven't. But I have a reason. I don't know if her mother has told her what she has up her sleeve, and I'm afraid if Glenda and I can't resolve this on our own, Carly will be dragged through the court system. You know sometimes they talk with the child to see what they prefer."

"Are you afraid of what she might want?"

Shame crept along his spine. Maybe it was his fear, but… "I'm not sure if that's my concern or if I don't want her to face a judge and feel cornered with both of her parents staring at her waiting for her response."

El nodded. "I understand what you're worried about, but I think the judge and other representatives talk with her privately. You and—what's her name?—Glenda wouldn't be there. Still, I can't blame you for not wanting to put her through that."

Rick gave a faint nod, his mind trailing off in a multitude of directions. He'd avoided an even deeper concern that worried him. Was Angie's attraction to Carly more than her feelings for him? Shame jabbed his senses. He should love the idea that Angie had a deep love for his daughter. But he wanted to be loved as deeply in her heart. His fear stayed embedded in his thoughts. He couldn't bring that up today. Maybe never. He signaled the waitress for the bill, and when it arrived they rose and headed for the SUV.

As Rick pulled away from the restaurant, El continued as if he hadn't been interrupted. "I've been thinking. Proverbs makes a better point. 'Even a child makes himself known by his acts.' Watch how she acts as she faces the situation. Behavior often says more than words."

His pulse hitched. "You've made a point. Carly's feelings can be seen especially from her expressions. It makes sense to learn what I can that way."

El patted Rick's shoulder. "I'm glad to hear it. Do you realize how long it's been since I raised children? Mine are older than you are, so it's been a long time."

Rick couldn't help but grin. "Scripture is old, El, but it's still full of wisdom."

El chuckled. "So here's my final thought. We know for those who love God all things work together for good.

Keep that in mind. I know you're a good father, Rick, and you'll do the right thing. Lean on the Lord and add a bit of common sense with the love you have for your daughter. What's best for Carly? That's what you have to ask yourself. That's what's important."

And it was. He knew El was right. "Thanks. Remember the next time you offer to lend your ear someone may take you up on it." Rick patted his chest. "See what happened with me?"

El laughed again. "But I got a good meal in payment and a good time with a new friend. So, Rick, I still mean it. I'm here if you need me." He gave him a wink. "And I think that lovely lady down the block is always there for you, too."

He couldn't resist. "You mean Birdie?"

The comment turned on El's laugh button. He guffawed and held his belly. Watching him, Rick broke into his own laughter, relieved that the silly comment had released the tension he'd felt since he'd initiated their dinner together. "You gave me things to think about, and you're right. Carly needs to know what's happening, and I want to see if her mother's been open with her. Carly hasn't said a word, so I've treaded lightly."

"Wise, but find out and then act." El gave him a wink.

"Good idea, El. I'll do that." He turned onto Lilac Circle and pulled into El's driveway.

El opened the door and paused. "Rick, we both know Angie has a good heart, and I'd like you to tell her something when you're alone."

His stomach tightened. "Sure thing. What is it?"

"We all know Birdie across the street there." He gave a subtle swing of his hand, and Rick looked up, noticing a woman watching from the front window. "It's not easy to like the neighborhood reporter, but Angie befriended

Rema, as you probably know. I think she could get to know Birdie."

A sweet sensation rolled through Rick's chest. "I agree. I've felt her good heart more than once."

El gave a faint nod. "I keep thinking that maybe Angie could gather some thoughts from the Good Book and find a way to bring out the positives in Birdie. I suspect the lonely woman doesn't like herself very well."

"Really?" His gaze drifted toward the house, and when he spotted her again, he turned away. "I'll let Angie know what you said, El. If anyone can be a friend, it's Angie."

"She's a rare woman."

Rick's chest swelled.

El gave a nod. "You're a pretty good man, yourself. I like you."

"I like you, too. But then, who wouldn't?"

El shook his head before he stepped to the driveway and closed the door.

Rick glanced down the street and saw Angie's car pulling into the driveway. "Speaking of Angie, she's back from dinner and toy shopping with Carly. That means I'd better get over there."

El patted the car window. "Thanks again for dinner."

He gave El a wave and backed onto the street, then headed to Angie's while one thought and then another rolled through his mind.

Carly's exuberant yell let Angie know Rick had returned. "Daddy, we bought toys and I had spaghetti and we had a great big strawberry shortcake this high." Her hands spread a foot wide.

"Not quite that high." She gave Rick a wink. "But close."

Rick raised Carly into the air and gave her a hug. "Did you have a good time?"

She nodded and ran on like a raging river detailing everything they'd done and seen, leaving out her comments about her mother's trip. Angie wanted to let Rick know. She'd promised not to tell him Carly liked being at his house best, but she hadn't been asked not to mention the trip. She muzzled the desire for now. Later, when they were alone, she would. She opened the trunk and set the packages on the garage floor.

"Can I show Daddy our new games, Angie?" Carly darted to one of the shopping bags.

"You sure can, but I get to show him one of them." She gave Carly a wink, grasped one of the smaller bags and beckoned them to follow her outside. When they'd gathered around her, she pulled out the bigger ball from the plastic sack, grinning at Carly's cute name for it.

Rick grasped the ball and twirled it on his fingertip while Carly giggled and clapped her hands. "Now, this is what I call a real ball. Not that pitiful beach ball."

Angie laughed with them while Carly stood mesmerized watching her dad with the ball.

"Can we play outside tomorrow? Can I invite Kimmy?"

"Whoa!" Rick held up his hand. "Tomorrow's Sunday and we have church, and did you ever think that Angie might have plans of her own?"

Carly faced her, her expression filled with eagerness to hear her response. Angie's heart melted. "I don't have one thing to do tomorrow, and I think I would miss seeing you."

Carly's face shone with joy as she bounced around beside them.

"You can play with the ball for a while if you want."

She gave the child a hug. "Your daddy and I will sit on the porch so we can talk a little. Okay?"

Her firm nod answered the question. Rick tossed her the ball, and she dropped it on the ground and kicked it across the grass, checking to make sure they were watching.

She and Rick ambled to the small back porch, where she'd placed two canvas chairs the day the children had played there. She settled on one and Rick on the other. His eyes searched hers. She suspected he knew she wanted to talk.

"How did you make out with El? I've been thinking about that and hoping it gave you some ideas."

"The talk was enlightening. He said things I should have thought of myself, but I was too wrapped up in the problem to see clearly. Now I do. First, I need to know if Carly has any idea about her mother's trip. I'll have to call Glenda."

"No, you don't."

His head jerked up and his eyes bored through her. "What do you mean?"

"She told me today and she looked sad."

He didn't speak a moment as if weighing what she'd said. "She didn't mention it to me. That bothers me. I—"

"Don't take it personally, Rick. I don't know how much she knows except when we were talking about something else and it just led in that direction. She looked rather sad about it."

"But maybe the sadness has to do with her mother going a—"

"That's what I thought, but she told me her mother wants her to go, too. That's when she looked the most upset."

"If I bring it up, she'll know you told me."

"You can find a way to draw it out without saying anything about me. You'll figure it out."

"Angie, I need your motherly talents."

His eyes searched hers and sent a prickle of longing through her. If they were married she would act the way a mother should act, but now she could be stepping on toes, toes of the ones she loved. She couldn't hurt Carly by letting her know she'd told her secret.

She jerked herself back to his comment. "It's instinct, remember? I'm not sure I have a talent."

"I think you do." Rick slipped his hand over hers.

She rolled her hand upward and wove her fingers through his.

"And, by the way, El thinks you have talent, too."

Angie listened while he told her what he speculated about Birdie, and her pulse skipped. She couldn't believe El wanted her to become a friend of the woman. It was like asking her to spend the evening with a snake in her bedroom. As soon as the thought arose, she regretted it. "I don't know, Rick. That'll take a lot of work. I can't think of a way—"

"El suggested you find the way in the Bible."

The Bible? "I wouldn't know where to begin."

"Google."

His response triggered her laughter. "I guess you can find the answer to anything there."

He nodded. "What would you say if I invited you to church tomorrow?" He leaned forward as if to kiss her.

But she drew back. On top of her dilemma and confusion, she drew back. "Let me give it some thought."

Disappointment weighted his expression and tore at her heart. She'd hurt him because of her own fear and worry. If Rick meant as much as she believed, her behavior told a

different story. She gazed at him, wanting to spill out her sinful past and have him take her in his arms.

Did forgiveness happen that way? Her chest ached with sorrow.

Chapter Ten

Angie settled on her sofa, her laptop balanced on her knees, and hit her browser. She hesitated, hearing the children's voices from the backyard. After church, Rick had arrived as if nothing had happened. She'd feared she'd looked dumbfounded, but she'd managed to smile. Carly hadn't been able to wait a moment to invite Kimmy to play with the new ring-toss game. Rick had set up the game, and while he'd explained the rules and monitored their play, she'd sneaked inside to look for scripture to help her deal with Birdie. But she needed to look up verses to help her with her guilt and forgiveness.

El's request hung on her mind. He trusted her to be Birdie's neighborhood friend and perhaps make a difference in her life. The sweet man had no idea what he was asking, and she found herself praying for help. The awareness struck her. Years had passed since she had prayed for anything. Even when Cal had been killed riding his motorcycle, she had shown anger toward God. Prayer had been impossible. Why would God let her live with him like man and wife, and then take him away before she could salve her guilt? Whether a strong Christian or not, she had morals and values. Her body shuddered with memory. Even

before Cal's death, she'd sensed their relationship had been going awry. She'd allowed herself to do things she knew were against her own values, but she caved in to Cal's pressure of joining in. Instead of anger at God, she should have blamed Cal and herself for being weak and—

An agonizing sense of guilt crept through her like spider legs walking down her spine. She closed her eyes, knowing the Lord forgave but wondering how deeply she might have dug a pit so that He could no longer see her.

The computer tilted. She balanced it again and typed, "What does the Bible say about helping people who slander or bear tales?" She clicked the search button, and when links popped up, she chose one, having no idea what she would find. Her chest tightened as she scanned the verses. Phrases jumped out at her—*love your enemies, love your neighbor as yourself, do to others as you would have them do to you, soft words turn away wrath, willing to forgive whether they ask*... The options swirled in her mind, tangling and spreading into a collage of blurring colors.

She dragged her gaze from the screen and wiped moisture from her eyes. How could she do even one of those phrases? Love Birdie? Forgive? Speak softly? She bit her lip to keep from releasing the words boiling in her mind. Doing good was easy for God. But not for her. Birdie was acid to a wound.

Then she remembered what El had said. *Birdie doesn't like herself. Birdie needs a friend.* If anyone could do it, Angie could.

She shook her head to stop the voice. Maybe she could, but how?

Her skin prickled, and she raised her head. "How long have you been standing there?"

Rick ambled through the doorway, concern darkening

his face. "Only a minute. Are you thinking about Birdie or Carly?"

Her pulse skipped. "This time Birdie. El has asked me to do something that is too difficult, Rick. I'm afraid I'm going to disappoint him." She closed the lid on her laptop and slid it to the floor.

Rick reached for her hand and eased her from the sofa. She looked into his eyes, hearing her pulse thud in her temple. "I'm sorry."

"Don't be." He brushed his finger down her cheek and pushed away a straggling lock of hair. "Tuck it into your mind. Ideas may come, and you may feel differently."

"I don't know how. No one likes Birdie."

"El sees her sorrow and vulnerability. You're perceptive. Think of it that way."

His determination caused a faint grin to curve her lips. "You're one of the kindest men I know."

His eyes probed hers. "Is that all?"

"No. But I don't want your head to get too big for your hat."

"I don't wear hats, so you're safe."

He moved as if to smile and instead she sensed his motion had more serious plans. His lips sought hers, a hungry kiss that opened doors and windows to her heart. Why couldn't she accept the happiness Rick and Carly had brought to her life? She slipped her hand along his back to the nape of his neck, feeling the softness of his hair, and she cupped his head, encouraging him to prolong the kiss.

She drew away breathless as her eyes sought his. "What are we going to do, Rick?"

"Throw caution to the wind as a bird would who found freedom at last."

"Daddy?" They jumped apart and spun around to face

the archway. Carly stood staring at them, her jaw sagging with a stretched smile on her lips. "Did you kiss?"

Disbelief caught Angie by surprise as it must have Rick. They burst into laughter at the same time as Rick opened his arms to Carly. She ran to him and jumped into his waiting embrace.

"Do it again." She looked from one to the other. "It looks pretty."

"Pretty." Angie fought to keep the titter from her voice. "That's a sweet way to say it, Carly." Her mind spun with panic, wanting to change the subject. What if Carly mentioned the kiss to Glenda? "Are you having fun outside? We were just going outside."

"We want to play with the ball now." She wiggled and Rick set her down. "Can we?"

Angie gave her a wink. "You mean the bigger ball, right?"

She nodded. "Not the beach ball." She wrinkled her nose.

"I think we've retired the beach ball now that you have the new one." Rick gave Angie a furtive glance, letting her know he was thinking what she had. "Let's go out and get the ball."

Rick and Carly charged through the archway to the kitchen while she stood a moment to get her bearings. If Carly told her mother about the kiss, Rick's chance to win in court could end in loss. To get her way, Glenda might blow the incident out of proportion. Glenda liked to win. This time Angie didn't stop herself from prayer.

While Carly got ready for bed, Rick paced the living room, struggling with the amazing kiss that had become an issue now that his daughter had spotted them. The next subject on his mind was how much Carly knew about her mother's trip. The two situations wrangled in his mind.

His brain had knotted into a lump of concern and confusion. It tethered his common sense, something El said he needed to use.

He blew out a stream of air and sank onto the sofa. If he asked Carly not to say anything about the kiss, he feared the request would make it even more exciting to share with her mother. If he ignored it, she might blurt out the information without thinking. Her glowing face filled with curiosity and pleasure gripped his mind. Carly wanted Angie and him to be a couple. He recognized her desire without her saying it. Her natural admiration and love for Angie showed more than words.

He felt the same. He admired Angie more than he could say and wanted her as his wife, but did Angie really want him? At times he was certain. Her kisses were as eager as his and her feelings for Carly were evident, but then she sometimes drew back as she had the day he'd asked her to go to church. A cold chill ran through him. Could it be Carly she loved, and he was only the add-on that came with his daughter? Something was holding her back, and his fear grew. To be part of Carly's life meant he came along for the ride. Would she take him on for that reason? He froze with the speculation. Could it be something else? Angie had steered away from offering details of her past. Which was it? Was she afraid to talk about her past or was it loving Carly more than him? He stared through the window into a night as dark and brooding as his spirit.

The thump of footsteps alerted him, and he planted a pleasant look on his face and watched the doorway. Carly come bouncing in and flopped beside him on the sofa. "I had fun today. I don't know any kids around here, but Angie has Kimmy." She flashed him a grin. "It's fun to play outside, and Kimmy's nice. I like her."

"I'm glad you have fun. You have fun at home with your mom. You have friends there, too."

She wrinkled her nose. "Robbie lives next door, but he's in first grade and he doesn't like girls." She lifted a shoulder. "And Dulcie moved."

"Then what do you do when you're with your mom?" She had more time there than with him. His chest tightened with longing.

She shrugged. "I'm at day care most of the time, so I have kids to play with there, and Miss Sally is nice." She wiggled around to tuck her feet beneath her. "When Mom picks me up, we have dinner, and then she tells me to read my books or play with puzzles." She lowered her head before tilting it up to look at him. "Do you know what that means, Daddy?"

"I'm not sure what you're asking me, sweetheart." He sorted through her words. "You mean do I know what *read your books and play with puzzles* means?" The question made no sense.

She gave him an exasperated look. "It means to be quiet."

Her look and explanation struck his funny bone, and he laughed.

Though she gave him an odd look, her eyes brightened and she laughed, too. "That's funny."

"You're funny. You make me laugh, and I love it."

"Me, too, Daddy." She snuggled against him. "Did Mom tell you about her trip?"

His stomach hit his lungs and hitched his breath. "She mentioned it." He bit his lip, wanting to ask questions, but he controlled his need to learn more.

"She wants me to go, too."

"She said something about it."

"I asked her why, 'cause she's going there to work. What will I do?"

He swallowed, overwhelmed by his frustration. He wanted to be honest and tell her he didn't want her to go. Yet he didn't want to sway her thinking. "Ask your mom, sweetheart. I don't know for sure. She'll probably find a day care for you while she's working."

"I have a day care." Her volume rose on the word as she tilted her head. Her eyes searched his. "I know the kids at my day care, and they speak like me, Daddy. In other countries, I don't know how to say their words."

"I don't either, but in most big cities people can speak different languages. That's what Europe is like. Many people speak English."

"I like Owosso. This is where I live."

He drew her into his arms. "I like you in Owosso, too, Carly, but your mom thinks you'll have new experiences and—"

"I can have new speriences when I'm seven. Okay, Daddy?"

Despite his sorrow, he grinned. "Seven sounds good to me."

She hugged him tightly and buried her head in his arm. "Tell her." Her head tilted upward, her eyes pleading. "Okay?"

A ragged breath ripped from his body. "Carly, you need to talk to your mom." He kissed her cheek. "It's time for bed, but I'll come in with you if you like, and we can say your prayers."

She gave a slow nod. His heart rending, he lifted her in his arms and carried her to her bedroom. Tonight wasn't the time to worry about the kiss and what she might say to her mother. He had more important things to worry about, and his daughter was number one.

* * *

Angie stared at the fresh batch of snickerdoodle cookies and bit the inside of her lip. Rick planned to talk with Glenda today while Carly was at day care, and she feared the worst. She'd paced since she'd arrived home from work, and to waste time, she'd decided to bake cookies. The cookie idea had struck her as a reason to visit Birdie, but the more she thought about it, the more she preferred something less concocted than cookies. Nothing struck her. Her stomach fell and rose as if inside a plunging elevator. She sank into the closest kitchen chair.

Instead of the baked goods for Birdie, perhaps it would be wiser to stop at El's, give him the treat and beg out of the task. She lowered her head, tried to make sense of her discomfort. When she thought about it, she didn't remember ever seeing company at Birdie's. The woman was lonely. Enough of her excuses.

She steeled herself, grasped the container and forced herself out the door. Before she reached the sidewalk, Rema waved to her. She stopped and waited for Rema to cross the street.

"Did you notice our new neighbor moved in?"

Angie glanced down the street and spotted a car in the driveway.

"I think she's single. I didn't notice a man other than a few who helped her move, but it looked as if no one stayed." Rema widened her eyes. "Sorry. I sound like Birdie."

Aware of her cookie container, Angie didn't know how to respond. She should tell her where she was headed, but with Rema's comment, she'd probably make her feel bad. She smiled and kept her mouth shut.

"Looks like you have another goody supply for Mr. Barnes." Rema motioned to the container.

Angie winced, cornered whether she wanted to be or

not. Part of her longed to nod and let Rema think that was where she was going, but that would be untrue. "Not this time. Believe it or not, I'm going to Birdie's."

"Birdie's." She staggered back a step. "You're kidding. Why?"

El's request faltered on her lips. "She's lonely, and I thought maybe—"

"A lot of us are lonely, Angie, but we're not vicious."

"I know." Scripture flew through her head, but she wasn't comfortable quoting the Bible. Not yet. She squirmed under Rema's questioning eyes. "El thinks she doesn't like herself very well." She held up her hand. "I know. We understand why she shouldn't like herself, but maybe something can break through her hurtful gossip."

"You really think so?" Rema's frown deepened. "She latched on to me last week with concocted tales." She faltered and looked away. "She might be right." She raised her head and shrugged. "Most likely she is, but it's not her business."

Angie worked to understand Rema's cryptic discussion. "What concocted tales?"

"Can't you guess?" She drew in a ragged breath. "After my serious discussion with Trey, Birdie said she saw him out with a woman. I don't see her go anywhere, so where would she have been?"

"Do you remember when Birdie told me the same thing about Rick? She'd been to dinner with her cousin and saw him with a woman." Angie faltered, realizing she hadn't talked with Rema since his sister's visit.

Rema shrugged. "You didn't tell me about that, and I'm glad it was only her misjudgments. But in my case, that's what I've always told myself, Angie, but I saw him. Remember? Each day the truth becomes clearer. I've confronted him once. His promises are empty, and I've waited long

enough. He's stifled me from living my own life while he's out carousing. He doesn't want me to work. I know why. Because then I'd be independent. This way he thinks I'm trapped. He tells me not to join the ladies' clubs because they're all gossip groups. Now I realize what he fears. Someone might have seen him out with a woman and knows he's running around. He's concerned I'll find out. I'm his convenient housekeeper."

Fighting to keep her jaw from sagging, Angie listened without response. "I wish I had the answer, Rema, but this is a decision you have to make on your own."

"I have the answer, Angie. Finally. I'm not going to live this way. I'm alone anyway, and it's time I gained some pride and confidence instead of living the life of a cleaning lady." Tears sprang to her eyes. "That's what I feel like."

Angie rested her hand on Rema's shoulder, wanting to hug her, but she could only guess that Birdie was at the window creating a new tale to spread. "Have you seen a counselor or—"

"I talked with an attorney. It's too late for counseling. Trey wouldn't be willing to go with me and going alone isn't what I need. I see things clearly now. I'm tired of fooling myself and giving him second chances." She brushed the last of the tears from her eyes. "I don't even love him anymore. I try but I can't."

Angie gave her shoulder a squeeze. "If you need an ear, Rema, please call on me. We all need listeners. It's lonely talking to ourselves."

A faint grin touched Rema's lips. "That's true. Thanks."

Seeing Rema's desperation, she gave her a quick hug and backed away.

Rema's eyes welled with tears. "You'd better go. I know you're on a mission." She tilted her head toward Birdie's.

"Good luck. If anyone can save the world, you can, Angie, but don't ask me to help. I don't have the energy."

Angie could only nod. She wiggled her fingers in a wave and trekked down the street, her mind shifting to Rick, an amazing man whom she trusted without question. If only Rema could have a love like that.

Love. Her pulse hitched. Their friendship had become a deep kinship that had grown and bound them together. Yes, her job could be in jeopardy, but she didn't care. She would deal with her company's antiquated rule when the time came. If she could speak from her heart and admit her sins, with Rick's forgiveness, she would open the door to the love and life she wanted with Rick and Carly.

As she neared Birdie's house, Bible verses came to mind. Even if she followed the scripture, she couldn't earn her way to heaven. But at least she hoped to honor El's strong faith. She glanced across the street at his house and released a pent-up breath as she faced her mission. No one ever said being a Christian was easy.

With all the fortitude she could muster, she walked up the sidewalk to Birdie's porch and rang the bell. She waited, shifting her feet and clutching the container. Deciding the bell might be broken, she knocked and waited.

After a minute and another knock, she lowered her shoulders, easing the kinks between her shoulder blades. "I tried, Lord. Thank You for the reprieve." After waiting a moment longer, she bounded down the steps and headed home, eager to talk with Rick.

When she walked into the house, she set the cookies in the kitchen, telling herself she would take care of the Birdie situation another day. She checked the time and sent a text message to Rick, hoping she wasn't catching him at a bad time. When no response came, she guessed he was still busy.

Instead of brooding, she grabbed a diet pop and stepped onto the back porch. Her flower beds were flourishing. Though the lilacs had faded and died, the roses now took their place with delicate beauty. The flowers Carly had helped plant were thriving, too, but so were the weeds. She curled her nose.

She set her drink and cell phone on the edge of the porch and slipped into the garage for a small trash bag and her garden gloves. Starting with the annuals, she weaved her way through the plants, plucked out the fast-growing weeds and dropped them into the plastic bag. Perspiration beaded on her forehead, and she brushed it away before stepping back to view her work. Not bad.

Moving to the roses, she was pleased to see only a few weeds had sneaked into the mulch. She bent down and jerked a couple from the ground as a shadow fell across her. Lurching around, her heart skipped. "Rick. I texted you a short time ago and—"

"I was on my way here." He drew her into his arms and let out a chuckle. "Nice effect."

She couldn't quite decipher what he meant.

He touched her forehead. "You have an earthy decoration right here."

Grinning, she turned the dirty glove to the back and rubbed it across her brow. "Better?"

He nodded and kissed her forehead. "I assume you were wondering how the talk went."

"You assumed right. What happened?" She pulled off her gloves, took his hand and led him back to the porch, where she took a seat.

He sank into one of the chairs and gave a heave. "Not great. I'm sure you expected that."

"But I hoped I was wrong." Though disappointed, she

now grew sad seeing his concern. "I'm sorry, Rick. What's the outcome?"

"First she accused me of putting ideas in Carly's head."

"You would never do that." Her pulse escalated. "Why would she say that?"

"She wants to blame someone other than Carly, and I'm the logical cause. Apparently Carly asked her why she had to go to Europe. I suppose she gave her the same arguments she gave me." He shook his head, releasing a jagged breath. "It's breaking my heart, Ang."

"I know." She wove her fingers through his. "No matter what she says, Glenda has to know better."

"Maybe." He shook his head again. "Carly's too smart for her age." He gave her the first grin she'd seen from him. "Since she can't get beyond her desire not to go, our next step is the representative from Friend of the Court."

"Does that concern you? I know you would have liked to settle this with Glenda."

"She's jumping for her attorney to get involved. She knows courts lean toward the mother, but I have to trust that someone will make sense of the situation and listen to Carly."

"But you didn't want her to get involved, Rick. That would mean—"

"I know." He looked defeated.

"If it's the only way, then let them talk to her. She's honest and they'll learn the truth."

"Glenda's pushing for action. Her trip is getting close."

"Getting a passport for Carly would be tricky." She rose and beckoned him to follow her inside. She went through the door, and when she stepped in, she fell into his arms, allowing her own feelings to release. They stood in silence for a time until Rick tilted her head upward. "I never

thought I would find someone like you, Angie. Never in a million years."

He lowered his lips to hers, and the hunger in her stomach could not compete with the depth of her longing to let him know how she felt. But she couldn't until she told him the truth. "I'm a woman who has always loved her independence, who never thought she would be a wife or mother, but being with you has changed me." She gazed into his eyes. "I want to be a new me, Rick, and I'm getting there. I just need a little more time."

Though a flicker of disappointment reflected in his eyes, their lips met again, and this time she felt the nudge of complete happiness and the feeling of hope.

Chapter Eleven

"That's not accurate, Mrs. Turner." Sitting in a small sterile office at Friend of the Court, Rick fought to maintain calm. "Carly asked me to talk with her mother, and I told her she should tell her mother how she felt. I would not coerce my child. She's upset enough."

Glenda leaned forward and slapped her palm against the tabletop. "She's upset because you're coaching her."

"Mrs. Jameson, please remain calm. I'm trying to get a picture of what you want and what Mr. Jameson wants."

Rick wanted out of there. He'd been hammered by Glenda's acerbic comments since they'd arrived. As with all her accusations, blaming him for Carly's desire to stay home from Germany was a fabrication.

"If you can't come to an agreement my hands are tied. I will suggest that this goes to court for a judgment. I'm not the law here. I'm your Friend of the Court representative for resolving issues without attorneys."

Rick's head drooped forward. "Please, Glenda, can't we resolve this without Carly being dragged into court? Neither one of us wants that."

Her eyes narrowed. "You don't want it because Carly

will tell the judge the truth. She'll admit that you told her what to say."

He tossed his hands into the air, unable to fathom her degree of determination. Though tempted to give up rather than make Carly be part of the ridiculous disagreement, he let the option drop. Carly's sad face rose in his mind, and he could still hear her pleading for him to explain to her mother why she didn't want to go.

Releasing a deep sigh, he studied the rep from Friend of the Court and prayed she hadn't believed Glenda's accusations. "Mrs. Turner, would it be possible for you to talk with Carly and perhaps come to a decision that way?"

The representative pressed her lips together, her eyes sweeping from him to Glenda. "Can I have an agreement from both of you on this?"

"Only if you talk with her at my home." Glenda's pitched voice gave away her attempt to control her anger.

"That's fine." Rick's concern about Glenda's pressure rose, but he knew his daughter. "Carly would be truthful no matter which home."

Mrs. Turner studied him a moment and then Glenda. "Let me call you in a day or two, and hopefully we can set up a visit. I will speak only with Carly. That means alone."

Glenda huffed, but didn't argue. "Can you do this quickly? I have to leave soon, and I need to obtain Carly's passport." She turned her head slowly toward him. "My former husband has been unwilling to sign the document."

Rick kept his voice level. "Since I'm responding on Carly's wishes, Glenda, I haven't signed it. If Carly decides she wants to go with you, I will sign it whether I personally want to or not. And you know if this were a vacation we would be dealing with a different situation. You're going to Germany to work. Carly will be cared for by strangers for much of the day."

"Let's stop here." Mrs. Turner stood. "I need to check my schedule, and I will call you, Mrs. Jameson. I don't work on your time schedule. I work on mine."

Rick rose and extended his hand. "Thank you. I think speaking with Carly in her mother's home will be less frightening for her than in a courtroom."

"You're welcome, Mr. Jameson." She gave a nod and turned her attention to Glenda, who finally stood. "I'll call as quickly as I can."

Glenda gave a halfhearted nod and grasped her handbag. "I hope so." She turned, opened the door and left.

His eyebrows shot upward, and he tugged them down. "Thanks again." He slid his chair back into place and strode from the room, his heart in his throat. If Mrs. Turner had any sense of right or wrong, she would see where the fault lay. He knew he wasn't perfect. He made tons of mistakes, but he loved his daughter more than himself. How could he agree to let her go when she said she wanted to stay home?

Angie's stomach knotted when she spotted Rick pulling into the driveway. His scowl showed through the windshield, and she guessed the result of the meeting. "What happened?" She pushed the door open, fearing he'd feel worse if she told him the whole story about herself. Burying her fear, she stood back to let him in. Her stomach knotted, her imagination twisting the two fears into hopelessness. "I can see you're not happy."

He ran his fingers through his hair and sank into the nearest chair. "Not very, although I did get a small option of hope."

She settled across from him and listened to a review of the meeting, her heart drawn into a whirlpool of despair. "So what happens now?"

"I suggested before court action Mrs. Turner, the Friend of the Court rep, talk with Carly to hear what she wants from her lips rather than mine or her mother's."

A wave of optimism washed through her. "And she will?"

He shrugged. "She'll call Glenda to make arrangements. Glenda wanted it at her house."

"So she can coerce Carly, I suppose."

Rick lowered his head, his response a mumble. "I hope not. She loves Carly despite her forceful manner. I'd like to think she'll let that override her own desire to win."

Angie wished she had the same confidence, but then, she didn't really know Glenda at all. Her opinion was based on her own interpretation of the woman's actions. "I hope you're right. Let me get you a drink. Something cold?"

His deep sigh swept into his response. "No, thanks. I need to do some grocery shopping and a few things around the place. I'll come back later if that's okay."

"You know it's okay. I wanted to talk with you about Carly's birthday."

His head shot up. "Can you believe I almost forgot about that with everything else on my mind?"

"But I didn't. I want to give her a surprise party...just to cheer her a little. She's looked stressed for a child and that breaks my heart."

He rose and took her hands. "Mine, too. I hope Glenda really looks at her and sees the reality of her decision."

"I'll pray for it, too, Rick."

His eyes widened, and he drew her into his arms. "It's wonderful to hear you say that, Ang."

"I'm a slow learner at some things but not hopeless."

Tension eased on his face and his lips turned into a faint grin. "You're never hopeless."

He drew her closer, his eyes searching hers as his lips

lowered to her mouth. She shuddered in his arms, though her concern remained heavy. Even the birthday party hadn't lightened her thoughts, but it would. God's will be done, but she sensed Carly would be there for her special day, and they could have a really joyful party.

He eased back and brushed his fingers along her cheek. "Don't worry, Angie. I trust that the best will happen if God is in charge."

She wanted to be as confident as he seemed, but she would pray knowing that with God all things were possible.

He hugged her and kissed the top of her head. "I'll see you later."

She nodded and grasped the door handle as the bell chimed. A frown interfered with her moment of contentment. "I suppose I have to answer."

"I'm leaving anyway, so the door has to open unless I sneak out the back."

The bell rang again, and she pulled open the door. Her heart rose to her throat. "Birdie. Hello." Though Birdie was an older woman, short and somewhat trim with a larger bosom, Angie could see a hint of youthful good looks. Yet today her puckered expression gave her face a shriveled look.

Rick eased past Birdie, who stood as close to the opening as she could get. "Excuse me. I'll let you ladies talk." He gave a wave and a sympathetic glance that Birdie couldn't see. "I'll see you later."

She stood a moment caught in a whir of confusion before returning to Birdie. "Come in." She pushed the door farther open. Although Birdie hesitated, she stepped inside while Angie faced the situation. She'd put off the visit and today Birdie had come to her door. She motioned her

to the living room. "Have a seat. Would you like something to drink?"

"No, this isn't a social call." Birdie gave her a haughty look blended with a hint of curiosity. "That man is still hanging around, I see." She shook her head, her tight gray curls giving a slight bounce. "Apparently you don't heed anyone's advice."

"I don't recall any advice, Birdie. Remember Rick and I are good friends, and the woman you told me about was his sister. I met her. She's very nice. I wish you could have met her, too." Slight exaggeration, but she'd said it in the name of being positive with the woman.

"Why would I want to meet her?"

Angie shrugged. "You seemed interested in her the day you saw her with Rick. I thought perhaps you'd like to tell her how pretty you think she is."

Birdie's startled expression took a moment to fade. "Well, that's not the reason I came here."

"Oh." She managed a smile. "Do you want to tell me why, then?"

"You were snooping around my house. Someone told me."

"Snooping?" She managed a smile. "Not quite. I came over with some homemade cookies I'd baked and thought I would share some with you since I admire how you keep a watch over the neighborhood." *Oh, Lord, forgive me for another exaggeration.*

"Cookies for me?" She faltered back a step. "But…"

"Maybe you don't know how nice it is to have someone keeping watch as you do. I assumed you were being a thoughtful neighbor." The more she talked, the greater her guilt. "Or are you looking outside for some other reason?"

Birdie looked at her, speechless. She finally relaxed her jaw. "I'm…curious."

"Curiosity is a good quality when you're doing it for the good of the neighborhood. The Lord tells us to watch over each other and to help people without receiving a reward because our reward will be in heaven."

Birdie flashed a questioning look. "I'm not a churchy person. My family didn't attend."

"Believing is the most important, Birdie, living your life for the good of others. I know sometimes people are…" Angie feared treading where she was headed. "Sometimes people are lonely and so they struggle with others' happiness. But no one finds happiness that way. Happiness comes from inside and from reaching out to others and following the Golden Rule. 'Do to others as you would have them do to you.'"

Birdie's face puckered as if she were trying to swallow a hunk of tough meat.

"You've heard that before, haven't you?"

She nodded.

"So thank you for your watchfulness." She took a step toward the kitchen. "I saved your cookies. They're in the freezer, but they're still good." She hurried away, catching her breath and praying the Lord had guided her words. She grasped the container, found a plastic grocery bag and slipped it in and then returned to the living room. "I hope you like snickerdoodles." She extended the bag.

"Don't know as I've ever had them." Birdie eyed the bag a moment before accepting it. "I've never had anyone give me cookies."

"Then it's about time." Angie smiled and waited.

Birdie held the sack in her hand as if waiting for it to do something.

Angie scuffled to break the silence. "You know who likes cookies? Mr. Barnes. El. He lives across the street."

Birdie nodded. "He's civil."

"El is a wonderful man. Has nothing but nice things to say about people. He mentioned how you look out for the neighborhood."

"He did?" A dubious look spread across her face. "I—" Faltering, Birdie seemed at a loss for words. "Sorry I said you were snooping. I guess you'd come with the cookies."

"I had, but no harm." She took a step toward the door. "Thank you for dropping by. I hope you enjoy the cookies."

"I will." She took the hint and headed outside. "Maybe I should buy some for... No, I should bake some for Mr. Barnes."

"That would be lovely. El would appreciate that. He misses his wife even though she's been gone awhile."

"Life can be lonely." Her head bobbed as she made her way to the sidewalk, and before turning, she paused and looked back. "Have you met our new neighbor?"

"No. Have you?"

"Not much happening down there. She seems to keep to herself. I've only seen her outside when she's getting into her car." She paused and pressed her lips together. "Maybe she has a lonely life, too."

"Maybe she does, Birdie." She watched Birdie turn away with a thoughtful look on her face and continue toward her house.

Angie gave a relieved sigh. She had no idea what she'd said to the woman, but Birdie's attitude had taken a one hundred and eighty degree turn for the better. Yes, it would take work, but it was work for everyone to change. Birdie was a work in progress. Angie stood a moment watching the woman meander down the sidewalk before she stepped inside, her mind turning again to Rick and his struggle. If only she had the right words to help him. The right words? Her own struggle ballooned in her mind. She needed the right words to admit her sinful past and to beg Rick's for-

giveness. The Lord forgave her. She'd learned that. But she still didn't trust human nature to forgive. Rick's nature was to put the best result on everything. He'd dealt with his personal difficulties without giving up and while looking for the best solution. She could do that if he really loved her. She sensed he did. She had one hope, to put it in God's hands. The only thing she could do was pray. Though still new at it, it was the best answer.

Rick bounded up Angie's steps and gave a knock before trying the door. It opened, and he leaned inside. "Angie, it's me."

"Come in, Me." She came through the archway with a grin. "You sound a little more relaxed."

He arched his brows. "I'm trying to be positive. While I was home, the rep called. She has an appointment tomorrow evening with Carly at Glenda's."

Angie's smile faded. "Worried?"

"I have no idea what will happen." He sank onto the sofa cushion. "If Carly tells the truth, I have nothing to worry about, but if Glenda says something that causes Carly to be afraid to admit her feelings, then I am worried." He exhaled, longing to take a full breath. He'd felt stifled since their earlier meeting. "I keep reminding myself that Glenda feels as I do. We both want our daughter with us. I guess we're both a little selfish, but I've tried to be fair, Angie. I've tried."

She settled beside him. "You're a good dad, Rick. Don't start doubting yourself. I think if this had been a regular vacation, you—"

"I told Mrs. Turner that. I wouldn't have been thrilled, but I would have agreed to the trip. I wouldn't deprive Carly of an exciting vacation even if she is only five. She's a smart five, and by the time she leaves, she'll be six."

Angie gave him a tender smile. "After her birthday, I'll miss her little reminder, won't you?"

He managed to grin back. "She'll remind us she's almost seven once she's six." He brushed Angie's soft cheek, longing to dislodge all his cares and revel in the amazing sensation he felt when she was in his arms.

"The problem is this is a business trip." Angie rested her head on his shoulder. "That's not a fun time for Carly. I'm sure she would be unhappy surrounded by strangers all day long."

He nodded, grateful she understood and wishing Glenda could see it that way.

"I know you're worried, Rick." She touched his cheek. "You'll know more tomorrow night."

His energy depleted, he managed a nod. He closed his eyes, wanting to sleep until the report came as to what Mrs. Turner would recommend. Sleep would make the time pass, and he wouldn't spend the waiting hours worrying.

His hopes and dreams for the future hit him head-on. What did he have to offer Angie? Nothing. This kind of life would plague him until Carly was of age. Maybe after that, too. He had no idea if Angie would accept a lifetime dealing with Glenda's wants and his excessive child support. Though he didn't begrudge the money for Carly, he resented paying so much when Glenda made far more money than he did. His thoughts buzzed like bees along with an occasional sting.

"You remember when Birdie arrived as you were leaving. Guess what happened?"

Pulling himself out of his doldrums, Rick opened his eyes. "In all this mess, I forgot." He shook his head, relieved Angie had dragged him from his negativity. "What happened?"

"I thanked her for being a watchful neighbor, one we could count on to see any problems in the neighborhood."

"You're kidding."

"No." She shook her head. "Birdie looked as startled as you do."

He chuckled. "You have to admit it was an interesting approach."

"But there's truth to it. If anyone tried to break in, Birdie would call 911 in a flash."

"I suppose she would." He listened while she described the conversation with Birdie. He was astounded at the faith Angie reflected in her comments. It inspired his sagging spirit.

"Birdie had a bounce to her step when she left. I know she won't change overnight, but I can hope it's a beginning."

"It's great, Ang. And we know that hope is a wonderful gift."

Her expression became serious. "I didn't have much hope before I really got to know you. Spending time with Carly, her perfect innocence, reminded me that as children we trust and hope for even the most impossible dream, believing it might come true."

"And they can, can't they?" He slipped his arm around her shoulders and drew her close, dodging his negative thoughts. "I have hopes and a dream, Angie. Three people are in that dream."

Her brow wrinkled. "Three?"

"Carly...and you with me. I dream we're a happy family, the forever kind."

She pressed her lips together, and he sensed she was about to weep. Instead she gazed into his eyes as her lips curved to a faint grin. "I have the same dream, Rick."

"You do?" He studied her while his pulse charged through his body.

"I do. Really. We have so much to talk about. Yes, we have problems to deal with, but they're not hopeless. We can overcome anything if we—"

"Care enough? And I think we do when I hear what you're saying."

She tilted her head, her eyes searching his. "I wish we had time to talk about it, but I'd like to wait and deal with the travel issue first. We both are thinking of that. Once we have the answer, we can enjoy sharing each other's hopes and dreams. I'm positive this will have a happy ending."

"How can you be positive?" She amazed him with her change in attitude.

"I did what you told me. Trust and let it go." She waited a moment as if in thought. "We have to do that, Rick." She drew herself upward. "Instead, let's plan Carly's birthday." She chucked him under the chin. "It can be here in the yard if we have good weather. We can have our families, Kimmy and Doug, if he wants to come. I might even invite El. I think that would make him happy."

"If you tell me you're inviting Birdie, I know you've gone off the deep end." He gave a full smile as her spirit renewed his.

"I don't think I'll go that far." She hopped up. "Let's do something. Get away for a while. Run, laugh. I don't care, anything that will help us feel wonderful and refreshed."

He rose beside her. "I have an idea."

"What is it?"

Though a phantom barrier remained between them, he drew her into his arms, his heart filled with love, his pulse racing as if he'd won a marathon. His lips met hers, his worries and doubts faded and happiness replaced all the negative thoughts he'd had. Angie would tell him even-

tually what blocked her admission of love. He believed it with all of his heart, and he would understand. Angie was right. Being strong and positive would get them both further than dragging their dreams in the mud.

Angie clung to him, her mouth moving beneath his, her heart beating in rhythm with his own, and he knew they would make it. He only had to have trust and hope. And pray.

Angie sat at her usual table in the company lunchroom, her focus on the door. Every time the handle turned, her heart rose to her throat. Another disappointment. An unwanted truth slipped over her imagining a day when Rick would come through the door a stranger. Her fear of another truth—her honesty—spread through her. Courage. That was all she needed. If their relationship was meant to be, her past would be gone and blessed with an amazing life with Rick.

She heard the door open, and this time she smiled from her heart as Rick stepped in. When she saw his expression, however, her smile faded.

He didn't head to the refrigerator as usual. Instead he plopped beside her and shook his head. "It's going before a judge."

"Rick, no. What happened?" The food she'd eaten wadded into a ball in her stomach.

"Apparently, Glenda wants the attorneys involved. She thinks Carly is saying what I want her to say."

"What did Mrs. Turner say? Does she agree?"

He dropped his face in his hands and massaged his forehead. "Who knows?"

Her jaw sagged hearing the tone of his voice. "The rep must have said something."

Rick lowered his hands and raised his head, his jaw

tight. "She has to stay noncommittal. It's part of her job. She can only propose a solution, and if the parties won't agree with her advice, her only choice is to recommend it go through our attorneys to the judge."

"Do you know what she suggested?" She pressed her lips together, controlling the urge to cry.

"I can guess. If she'd agreed that Carly should go to Europe, Glenda would have agreed with her decision. She didn't, so that answers the question."

She nodded, aware her heart had got tangled in her own desire. "Obviously. I should have seen that." She let his message sink in and tried to sort out what might happen now. "Do you have a date or know when?"

"We have to contact our attorneys. They'll set the date and let us know. I'm sure Glenda is pushing for action since she's going to have to jump through hoops to get Carly's passport in time to go if the court agrees with her."

Angie thought about praying that the date was delayed so she didn't have time to pursue Carly's passport, but prayers weren't to be selfish. She knew that much. She could only pray God's will and hers were the same.

"I called my attorney this morning. He knows the details, and he'll get the rest from Mrs. Turner. I'm sure it will be soon."

She glided her hand toward his and then stopped herself, noticing a table of coworkers was watching them. A desire to follow through with her action rose, but she squelched it, unwilling to add another problem to Rick's life or hers. "Then we wait. And pray."

A gentle smile touched his mouth.

She motioned to the refrigerator. "You'd better try to eat something before you get sick."

He lifted his shoulders. "I don't know if I can."

"Try. We have a battle to win, and you have to stay

strong and healthy." She struggled to keep from taking him into her arms and kissing away his fear.

His eyes said the same, but they could take no more chances than they'd already taken at work. People were speculating about their relationship, but it couldn't go further than that. Sealing the temptation to even touch him, she tilted her head, and his quick nod said he understood.

Angie couldn't let go of Rick's situation. She'd spent the day at work distracted, and now that she'd got home, she checked her cell phone every twenty minutes to make sure Rick hadn't called and she'd missed it somehow. Every time she heard a car on the road she jumped to the window, only to be disappointed.

When she calmed herself, reality settled over her. Rick had things on his mind, calls to make, household tasks to do, and he would call her when he'd heard something. Instead of wasting time, she thought of her new neighbor, walked to the front window and looked toward her house. The woman's car was in the driveway. Rather than appear at her door empty-handed, she grabbed scissors from the kitchen drawer and stepped onto the back porch.

Her roses abounded in the garden beds, and her snapdragons were in full bloom. She headed for the roses, selecting the freshest blossoms, and snipped off a few, pricking her finger in the process. Being more careful, she finished the rose bouquet and added a few snapdragons for color. She carried the bouquet inside and wrapped the base with plastic wrap, grabbed her house keys and stepped outside to meet the new neighbor.

The home looked something like hers although her front window was a double picture window and this one was a bay. The landscape was similar to hers before she had got

busy with her gardening. Now empty flower beds waited for loving hands.

The closer she came to the house, the less sure she became. Thinking back to Rema's visit, she hoped she could read the woman's body language better than Rema had read hers. She planned to welcome her, hand her the bouquet, point out where she lived and return home, and wait to hear from Rick.

She gave her head a subtle shake, longing to let those worries fade for a while.

After she rang the bell, the door opened with such speed she jumped. A young woman, attractive even with little makeup, gave her a curious look. "Can I help you?"

Angie managed to smile. "No. I'm your neighbor two doors down on the other side of the street." She swung her free hand in that direction. "I wanted to welcome you to Lilac Circle."

The woman's eyes widened. "Goodness." She eyed the flowers and opened the door wide. "Thank you. Would you like to come in?"

"I don't want to get in your way. I know how it is when you move. I've only been here three months, and I had boxes stacked around for a long time."

"I'm almost finished. Please." She widened the door and stepped back.

Surprised at the neighbor's welcoming expression, she accepted the invitation. "I'm Angie Bursten." She extended the flowers. "These are from my garden."

"They're lovely. I know my yard looks pitiful. The house was for sale for a few months, I think."

"It was. I looked at mine first and loved it, so I didn't check any further."

"I'm Nina Jerome. Single. Now." She gave her a faint grin. "That's usually the next question I get."

"Join the crowd." Angie pondered her "single now" comment. "My mom and sister were determined to introduce me to every single man they'd ever met no matter how much I protested."

A questioning look slipped to her face. "You said they *were* determined. How did you get them to stop?"

"I sort of fabricated a story. I told them I was seeing someone, but that sort of wove itself into a spiderweb. They wanted to meet him and it never stopped. I lied."

Her shoulders sank. "They're back at it, then."

"No." Rick's image filled her mind. "A coworker pretended to be the guy, and now he is the guy. Amazing how things work out."

"That's awesome." She lifted the flowers and beckoned her to follow. "I'd better put these in water."

Angie strode behind her into the kitchen. "From your comment, I assume you were married once."

She pulled a vase on an upper shelf of her cabinets. "I was."

"He died?" Angie felt as if she had to drag the words from her mouth.

"No. Divorced." Nina turned her back and filled the vase with water.

Angie sensed she'd made a mistake asking. "I'm sorry, Nina."

"I was sorry too once. I'm pretty much over it now." She placed the flowers in the vase and began arranging them into a bouquet.

Angie wasn't sure if she should drop the subject or get it all out. Her mind flew to Rema, but she didn't mention an affair. "No matter what happened, I'm certain it was very difficult."

"If things had been different, it might have been easier." She turned around holding the lovely arrangement.

Angie stifled her curiosity and focused on the flowers. "Pretty, Nina." An idea flashed. "Our new neighbor down the street about six houses is single. He's caregiving a niece, Kimmy. Her mom was in a car accident somewhere and can't travel." Kimmy seemed to catch Nina's interest. "His name is Doug Billings." As she spoke, it struck her that she sounded like her mother and she winced.

Nina whipped her hand in the air. "Not me. My marriage was enough to end my interest in men for a lifetime. They come across as amazing, willing to stand up for you in every dire moment, but when the moment comes, they shrivel up like cowards, and poof, they're gone. Eventually he'll find another woman who has longer hair or is a year younger. I was dumped because I lost two babies."

"Oh, Nina, I'm so sorry. Two." She bit her lip, wondering how horrible that would be to expect the joy of a child and then lose it. "But don't give up on men. I had a bad experience, not like yours, but bad. Yet I healed." She caught her breath. For once, she expressed something that made sense. The old mountain from a molehill jarred her. Had she done that? Was her sin any worse than another? No one was sinless, not even Rick. The awareness caused her chest to constrict. "Finally I realized there are men who are what you see and what you love. Rick and I were friends first, and then I met his five-year-old daughter and fell in love with her first. Rick followed soon after." Her head spun with the admission, but it was the truth.

"Really?" She looked quizzical. "Does he know his daughter was the one that captured your interest in him?"

"It's never been spoken, but I think he does. That was one thing that drew him closer. He told me he'd met women who liked him but weren't so keen on a child. I never thought I would be, but the moment I met Carly, that was it. I was mesmerized." She noticed a few boxes in the cor-

ner of the kitchen. "I don't want to take your time. I know you still have things to unpack, but I wanted to stop by and welcome you to Lilac Circle. And if you have any questions about Owosso or the neighborhood—anything—just ask. I work during the day, but I'm home in the evenings and on weekends."

"Thanks so much. And thank you for the flowers. You've inspired me to get this job done." She swung her hand toward the stacked cartons. "Then I can get outside."

Understanding totally, Angie nodded and headed for the door, relieved that the visit had been pleasant and noting that she'd found a neighbor she felt a kinship to.

When she arrived home, she refused to pace any longer. Rick would call when he knew something. She repeated the new mantra a few times and busied herself with party ideas for Carly's special day. She and Rick had talked briefly, but she needed to set a date and send out invitations. As she bent over her list, she heard footsteps and her pulse skipped. "Rick?" She turned and saw him standing in the kitchen door. "Any news?"

"We go to court on Monday. Five days away. Naturally Glenda is irked since it's getting tight for her to get the passport, and if the judgment goes her way, she'll pay a much higher fee to rush the passport. She's angry at me for not signing, but if I do, you know what that means."

She nodded. "You wouldn't need a court hearing then. Glenda would have what she wants, though not what Carly wants."

He ambled toward her. "I miss you. Our friendship was great, but now it's natural and comfortable and…" He drew her into his arms. "And it's amazing."

She raised her lips to his, a natural, welcoming response to the hours she'd paced and longed to be with him. Her inability to accept their true relationship had shattered.

Easing away, she captured his gaze. "I met the new neighbor today, and I told her how much Carly means to me. I mentioned that I'd fallen in love with Carly first, and she asked if I told you that." She tilted her head. "You realized that, didn't you?"

A tender grin touched his lips. "You were obvious, Ang. That sealed the deal. I figured if you'd been mesmerized by Carly, eventually you'd feel the same about her dad."

She nuzzled her cheek against his chest. "You were right, and it wasn't eventually. It was almost immediately, but I didn't want to admit it."

"I know." He tilted her head up and lowered his mouth to hers, this time sharing a lingering kiss that sent her heart to the heavens. "Angie, I don't have the words, except—"

"Shh." She pressed her index finger against his mouth. "After this mess is decided, Rick. We'll be ready to celebrate then. The court date is close."

He gave a sad nod. "Later."

"Will Carly go with you to court or—"

"I don't think so. We can leave her at day care, but if the court asked to talk with her, we'll need to get her there somehow."

"I'll take the day off, Rick. I can bring her over to the court and vanish. It won't be a problem at all."

"I can't ask you—"

"You didn't ask. I offered." She noticed his expression. "I know. Glenda won't like that because as you know I'll coerce her to—"

"I'll check with her, Angie. She wants this over with, and if it means getting Carly there quickly, she may agree. Glenda's mother doesn't drive and her sister—though not too far away—works, too. They don't see each other much, either."

"Then I'm the answer." But was she the answer in a

broader sense? Could she be the wife he deserved, one who was untainted, one who was pure?

He nodded. "You are."

Her stomach knotted. She wanted to hear more. Where was the kiss? Had she pushed him away too long and now was she only a convenience in his life?

Angie stood gaping as Carly bypassed the first landing and climbed to the second level of the Playscape tower. Without saying it, she'd apparently planned to come down the bigger slide. "Carly." Her heart caught in her throat. She swallowed, hoping to retrieve her voice. "Carly, be careful."

Carly waved and vanished from her sight. She ran to the side where the enclosed slide emptied and out shot Carly, laughing as she flew to the ground. She hit it with a thump, and though she could have been hurt, she bounded up and giggled.

Not wanting to discipline her with so much going on in her life, Angie helped her up and tucked her arm around her. "If you're going to do something up that high, Carly, we need to talk about it. Okay?"

She looked sad for a moment and then nodded. "I went too high."

"You did, but I'm happy that you didn't hurt yourself. I love you too much."

Her eyes brightened. "I love you, too."

She gave Angie a hug, and all her strictness melted away. She drew in a breath. "Should we let that be the last slide for the day?"

"'Cause I disobeyed?"

Carly's concerned look touched her. "No, because I wanted to talk with you, and we could get an ice cream and sit at a picnic table."

Carly clapped her hands. "Let's talk at the picnic table."

They headed for the car. Carly climbed into her booster seat, and Angie checked the seat belt before they headed down the highway. The only place she could think of was the Cone Zone on Water Street. The drive was short, and after they picked out their flavor choices and were handed their cones, they found an unoccupied table.

Carly slipped onto the bench, licked her cone, and when she glanced up, a concerned look darkened her face. "You said we would talk."

Angie had to muzzle her laugh. "Yes, I did." She gave her a wink. "It's about your birthday."

"My birthday." Carly's face brightened. "I'll be six, and I'll go to real school. First grade."

Angie grasped her napkin and caught the drizzle of ice cream running down Carly's cone. "You will. In first grade you'll really have fun homework then."

She nodded and took another lick.

"So, tell me what you'd like for your birthday. What kind of present?"

Carly looked into the air and thought a moment. When she looked up, her eyes had brightened. "Can it be any kind of present?"

Confused, Angie nodded, praying it wasn't a pony.

"Good. Then I want my present to be that I can stay in Owosso and not go to Germany."

Angie choked, touched by her requested gift. Unable to control her emotion, tears rimmed her eyes and blurred her vision. "I want that, too, Carly, and so does your daddy."

"Can I?"

"We'll see what the judge says." Angie's chest weighted.

"But I told that lady." Her lip trembled. "I told her why I wanted to stay with Daddy. She didn't believe me."

"No. I think she believed you, but—" She'd opened her mouth and now she had to end the sentence. "But she

can't make the decision unless everyone agrees, so the judge will decide."

"But I didn't talk to the judge."

"You…" She swallowed her empty words. "We'll see what happens, okay?"

"Daddy will tell them."

Angie bit her lip, sick of the struggle with Glenda and sick of herself and her ineptitude. Wrestling with her own thoughts had moved her no closer to the life she wanted. She adored Rick and loved his daughter. She was sick of waiting on herself to trust him and trust God. Bible verses in John's gospel flashed in her head. *"And the truth will set you free."* It was time to act.

Knowing Rick's forgiving nature, she had to trust that he would forgive her. Still, the fear that he might not tempted her to keep her silence. She wanted to be set free, and she could only be free with the truth.

As soon as Rick came through the courthouse door, he dug out his cell and hit Angie's number. His heartbeat charged through his body and pounded in his temple. He drew in the warm air and listened to the ring.

"Rick. What happened?"

"Ang, we won. The judge said it was a no-brainer." He chuckled. "Not in those words, exactly."

"Really." Hearing his spirited chuckle made her happy. "Hang on. I want you to tell Carly."

He heard a rustle and Carly's excited voice. "Daddy, can I stay with you?"

When he opened his mouth to speak, tears rolled down his cheeks. "Yes, sweetheart. Yes, I have custody until your mom comes back."

"Angie, Daddy has me until my mom comes back. Yeah!"

His chest ached with the pounding. "Let's celebrate tonight."

"Daddy." Her voice softened. "Did Mom cry when I couldn't go with her?"

Glenda never cried, or if she did, he never saw it. "She was upset, but the judge is the final say, and he said yes, so everything is okay, and Mom will adjust."

"Mom a'justs to things. Is she mad at me?"

"You? No. The decision was the judge's." He paused, not knowing how to appease her fears. "Let me talk to Angie a minute, okay?"

"Okay. I love you, Daddy."

"I love you, too, Carly." Emotion caught in his throat as he listened to the rustle of Carly giving Angie the phone.

"Rick. I'm so happy. How did it go?"

"I'll tell you when I get there. You know Glenda was irked, especially about child-support issues, but I think she'll face reality once she's on her way. We'll work it out. Carly can call her and she can call Carly."

"Are you coming soon?"

"As fast as I can get there."

"We'll be waiting."

He clicked off and bounded down the Corunna court-house steps. Not only was he eager to talk with Carly in person, but he wanted to waylay a confrontation with Glenda.

After he slipped into his SUV, he noticed Glenda heading his way. He backed from the parking slot and drove away as if he hadn't seen her. With all the tension the past weeks, he couldn't take dampening his joy again. God knew the truth and so did Carly and Angie. That was all he needed.

Traffic seemed slow as he headed toward Lilac Circle. Impatient, he took a side street and pulled into Angie's

driveway in good time. As soon as he turned off the motor, the door to the house flew open and Carly darted down the porch steps, her arms open. He flung back the door and scooped her into his arms. "I told you Mrs. Turner listened."

Carly's eyes widened. "Did she tell the judge I wanted to stay with you?"

Angie had arrived and appeared eager to hear his response. "She did. The judge said he had no need to talk with you since she had told him what you wanted. He agreed that you were better off here than being rushed off to Germany."

He paused, deciding if he should tell her the rest. The news made him happy and he hoped Carly would feel the same. "Your mom said she would be in Germany for at least a month. Is that okay?"

"A whole month?" Her grin blossomed and was matched by Angie's. "I'll miss Mom, but I'll be with you..." She turned her head and smiled. "And with Angie. I'm happy."

He drew her closer and gave her a giant hug, relieved that she had accepted her mother's plans. He set her down, his mind dealing with his suspicion. Something told him that Glenda had had plans to be gone a month all along. Maybe longer but hadn't admitted it.

Angie's shoulders lifted. "A whole month." She paused, looking at him with question. His face had given him away again. "At least the dispute has ended."

Carly's grin faded to curiosity. "What's a dis...a dis—"

"Dispute?" Rick tousled her hair. "That's a pretty big word, isn't it?" He eyed Angie, hoping she could save him.

"Dispute is sort of like what the judge had to do. He had to make a decision." She gave him a quick look as if asking if her response had been satisfactory.

Carly nodded. "Because if I had to be there a long time,

I would want to come home and that would be another dispoot."

"It would." He gave her a wink. "But now we don't have to worry. The judge said you're here until your mom comes home."

"I get to live with you now." She skipped down the sidewalk and back. If he hadn't been an adult, he might have joined her.

Despite his relief, he still had a challenge. Carly's belongings had to be moved to his house, and he hated the confrontation that was bound to occur.

Angie gazed out Rick's apartment window watching dusk lower in the sky and listened to the hum of Carly's prayers as he tucked her in. The days had passed in a blur of activity as Carly moved her clothes and toys to Rick's while Rick dodged Glenda's comments, but they'd both agreed it could have been worse. Once the judge had spoken, the disagreement ended—not ended exactly, but Glenda's few complaints had had nowhere to go.

Angie understood Glenda needed a way to vent her frustration. Although Angie disliked the woman, Glenda was Carly's mother and that meant finding positive attributes. The woman would be in her life from now on if she married Rick.

If she married Rick. The idea still twirled like strands of colorful ribbon, bright and lovely yet delicate. Angie feared the ribbons might snag and tear in the whirlwind of her excitement.

Her life plans had made a full turn. She'd pondered what she needed to do. She'd waited too long. The time had come to face what she'd dreaded. If Rick loved her and wanted her as his wife, he needed to know the truth about her life with Cal. She'd always feared the admission with any man

she might get serious with, yet knowing Rick, she sensed he would forgive her for the past... At least, she hoped it with all her heart.

The voices quieted, and she settled on the sofa, picturing Rick and Carly saying good-night. She had longed to go into the bedroom and listen, but this was a time of adjustment for Carly, and her presence didn't seem appropriate. Not yet.

Her pulse skipped as possibilities soared through her mind. She and Rick had agreed to hold off their discussion until Carly's problem had been resolved. And now it had. Her mother had flown out a few evenings ago after Glenda and Carly had said their goodbyes.

Rick had guaranteed Carly and Glenda the phone calls would be plentiful, and he even suggested video chats and offered to put one of the programs on his computer so Carly and her mother could see each other as they talked.

Hearing a noise, Angie swung her head to the doorway. Rick walked in carrying two mugs. "Coffee? I thought you might like a cup."

She nodded. "A good thought." She grasped the mug handle, took a sip and set it on the table beside her. "How did it go? I know it's been an adjustment, but is she really okay?"

"Better than I expected. She's a little sad about her mom leaving, but she thinks of the alternative and is happy again. Carly's so grown-up, Ang. I can't believe how well she thinks through things. I might have a little genius on my hands."

"That girl of yours takes after her daddy. She's loaded with common sense."

Rick set down his mug and sank beside her. "You think so? Sometimes I wonder if I have a brain."

She gave him a playful punch. "I'm sorry I keep asking how she's doing. I can't help but worry."

"Carly's strong and begged to stay in Owosso, so I'm confident she'll be fine. She'll miss her mom, especially as time passes. I have no doubt, but it's only a month…" He gave a shrug. "It's natural. I miss you when it's been a full day and we haven't been together."

She'd experienced the same longing to see him. "This week has been one of those, but I knew you had a multitude of things to do with Carly. Gathering her belongings, moving them to your place and settling the child-care arrangements, so many details. But I still missed you."

Rick shifted on the sofa and drew her closer. His eyes lowered to her mouth as his lips found hers. The gentle kiss lingered, sending her pulse galloping. Rick eased back, kissing the tip of her nose and touching her lips again before settling against the sofa cushion while keeping his arm around her. "I hope that lets you know that I missed you, too."

He leaned over and grasped his coffee mug. "We've won the battle, Angie. Our prayers were answered, and Carly is with me. It's something I wanted forever but never thought would happen. Believe it or not, I do feel sorry for Glenda. Despite her busy life and devotion to her work, she loves Carly in her own way, and she will miss her. I'll do everything I can to help them connect. I would hope that she would have done the same."

"You've been great, Rick, and I'm glad you have compassion for Glenda. I also love that you said we've won. That means the world to me. You know I adore Carly. I couldn't love my own child more."

An easy grin curved his lips. "That's another reason you mean so much to me, Ang. It's why I love you."

Her heart stopped beating for a fleeting moment, and she caught her breath. He'd never spoken the word *love* before, and she hadn't been prepared, but her own feelings rose to her throat. "I love you, too, Rick. I cherish you."

"Then that means…"

She touched his arm and nodded. "It does mean what you hope, but before you say anymore, I really need to talk with you."

His happiness turned to muddied concern. "What is it, Ang?" His frown deepened.

Her chest tightened, weighted by the admission she had to share. "It's nothing about you or my feelings, Rick. I want to be open with you. I need to put everything out on the table so one day you don't hear comments that disappoint you. And you need to know who I've been and decide if I'm the kind of woman you can still love."

"Woman I can still love?" Question filled his eyes. "Angie, what are you talking about? I don't understand. Were you in trouble or—"

"No. Not that kind of trouble, but I need to tell you about my life with Cal." Her throat caught as she shared her sorrow at giving herself to him without marriage, living a life she didn't believe in, though one she thought would bring her happiness and a successful marriage.

As she looked back over the years, her delusions sent her questioning her sanity. Her father had said who needed to buy a cow when the milk was free. The saying had angered her at the time, but her father had been correct. Cal had got what he'd wanted while she'd been left feeling dirty and empty as he'd gone off with his friends, usually dragging her along even though she didn't enjoy their company or their morals. Drugs. Alcohol. She'd been surrounded by it and had joined them on occasion, only to feel more degraded.

Rick rose, his eyes burning. "No more. Angie, I'm disappointed in you."

Her heart sank, her hopes and dreams shattered. "Rick, please." She swallowed a sob. "I—"

"Stop, Angie. Please."

Her heart plummeted to the depths of her being, and a sob lurched from her throat.

"Don't cry." He studied her with eyes that looked as if they were carrying the weight of the world. "I can't believe that you would think my feelings are so shallow. What kind of person do you think I am?"

Her eyes blurred with tears. "I wasn't judging you, Rick. I'm condemning myself. Back then, it wasn't the me I could be proud of. I—"

He touched her arm, drawing her up. "I can't bear to have you even think…" He closed his eyes and drew in a lengthy breath. "I love you, Ang. Not things that happened in your past."

"But I'd hoped you could forgive—"

Rick pressed his finger to her lips. "Forgive you? There's nothing to forgive. How would you even question my feelings?"

His eyes probed hers as her chest constricted.

"I love you for who you are now." A tender look flooded his face. "Do you think I've been sinless? I've done my own foolish things, and those behaviors weren't me either, but all my friends were doing it. It went against my beliefs and my values, but I wanted to be like my friends." He shook his head. "You're not alone. We're all sinners and, thanks be to God, we are forgiven."

She searched his face, realizing for the first time that love and forgiveness were one, the same as marriage, a union that was blessed by the Lord. How could she have allowed her fears to hold her back from the amazing experience of loving Rick?

He lifted her chin and tilted her head up, his eyes drawing her in. "Now, you have to forgive yourself." He lowered his lips to hers.

The kiss washed over her as if a baptism, cleansing her shame and sadness with Rick's undying love…just as the Lord had done.

"Rick." She gazed into his eyes. "Thank you for who you are and for who you've helped me become."

He studied her a moment before a grin played on his face. "Now, sweet Angie, can I ask that question?"

She smiled back, her heart filled with more love than she'd ever known. "Please. Ask."

"Angie, my best friend and soul mate, the woman of my dreams, will you be my wife?"

She flung her arms around his neck. "You know I will. Did you ever doubt it?"

He gave a faint shrug. "On occasion, but I kept nudging the Lord and He heard me." He wove his fingers between hers, drew her hand to his mouth and kissed her ring finger. "I'd like to make it official at Carly's birthday party on Saturday if it's okay with you? We'll have everyone there, and they can share in our happiness."

"I wouldn't have it any other way, and before we do anything, you should talk with Ca—"

"I asked her tonight, and I had to wrestle her to keep her in bed. She's happier than I've seen her since you bought her the bigger ball."

His sputter brought her to laughter. She wiped her eyes, trying to control her giggles, and knew this was the kind of life she wanted always. She slipped her arms around his neck again and lowered her lips to his, offering him the kiss she'd wanted to give him since the day she admitted to herself she loved him.

Rick grabbed his cell phone and tried to open his eyes. Who would call him at six in the morning? He forced his

eyelids wider and gaped at the caller. Questions flew as he pushed the talk button. "Glenda. Is something wrong?"

"No, not really, but—"

"It's six a.m. here."

"Sorry, I forgot the time change. I wanted you to know I have a change in plans."

His heart stood still. "You're coming back sooner?"

"No. I'll be staying here longer."

A sound caught in her throat and he realized it was something he rarely heard other than anger. "How long, Glenda? Have you considered Carly's feelings?"

"Yes, and that's why I wanted her here with me."

Fire rose up his chest. "You mean you knew you were going to be there longer and—"

"Rick, I wasn't certain how things would work out." A sigh rattled across the line. "Let me explain." She released another stream of air that puffed in his ear. "A while ago a coworker from Germany came to the States to work on a joint project. He had lived in the US for years. I knew him then, but he had moved back to Germany to be with his mother, who was in poor health. She died, but he'd settled in his job here, and…"

He waited, trying to piece together her rattled explanation to make some sense out of it. "And what?"

"We'd started dating, and I really liked him. John was like me, driven by his work and yet enjoying the comforts of life, too."

"So now what?" He guessed what was coming.

"He's asked me to marry him, and I said yes. I know it seems fast, but he was in the US for months a while back, and we've been on the phone since he left. I know this is it, but there's Carly."

"Yes, there's Carly, Glenda." A thousand questions spun in his mind. "How long will you be there?"

"I think I can work here for a while, and then we'll decide. If they won't keep me on, I'll find something else, but we're hoping we can both come back to the US eventually. John is willing to look for work there. He's very qualified and could get another job if it came to that."

Her words tumbled over each other without being sorted, and he knew being in love didn't always leave time to get a plan together. His feelings for Angie left him befuddled at times. "You'll figure it out, Glenda. I'm happy you've found someone, but my concern is Carly. When will you tell her?"

"I thought…I…"

Struck by reality, he grimaced. "You thought I should tell her for you. Is that right?"

"Rick, you're there. I don't want to ruin her birthday and call her then to break the news. If you tell her now, then she'll have time to… I don't know. She'll have time to take it in."

He stared into space, unable to decide how to deal with her request. "Has Carly met him? That would make her more prepared."

Silence. He knew the answer. "Glenda, why didn't this John guy meet her? She's your daughter, and he must have known you had a child." Horror struck him. "He did, didn't he?"

"Yes. He knew. But…"

"But he doesn't like kids?"

"Not exactly. He didn't want to be tied down to a pre-made life, and so I just let it go until he began to feel about me the way I felt about him. Now, yes, I want him to meet her."

"I'm not shipping her to Germany, Glenda. She's just beginning to adjust to being here without you. You don't expect me to—"

"No, I don't expect you to send her here, but we'll work out something."

His mind flashed. "I proposed to Angie yesterday, Glenda, and she said yes. Maybe I can bring Carly there on our honeymoon. Maybe you could take vacation time and have quality time with her while Angie and I have a little honeymoon time alone. Do you think—"

"That would be perfect, Rick." Relief filled her voice. "Would you do that for me?"

"I'll do it for Carly, Glenda. I know she'll want to see you and meet your new husband."

"Thank you, Rick."

"I'll keep you posted, and I don't like breaking the news to her. You could call back later when she's awake."

"It's not a good time. That's why I called now, and yes, I forgot about the time change."

"I think telling her is your…" His thought faded. "Will you call her on her birthday? It's in two days."

"I'll call her then."

"We're having a party at Angie's, so call on my cell." He gazed at the clock now reading six thirty. "She'll be anxious to talk with you, Glenda."

He heard a tremor in her voice. "Tell her I love her."

"I will." He ended the call, and dropping back on the pillow, he faced what he'd been asked to do. How could he break the news to Carly? A child needed to hear it from her mother. In the midst of frustration, he knew life would be better. He had a partner who understood what Carly needed—what he needed. Angie's unadulterated love completed his life. Her openness and expressions of joy and delight over becoming a family filled him with a wholeness he'd thought had been lost.

Since Glenda had put him in a bad spot, he would make the best of it. Yet if he didn't tell Carly, the news would

ruin her birthday, and he couldn't do that. He stared at the ceiling and prayed he would find a way to tell her that she could handle.

Angie rested her shoulder against the archway door and watched the interaction between her parents and Rick's mother. So far so good. Her sister, Connie, had latched on to Rick's sister, Rene, and they were sitting on the back porch watching the children play games. The men were participating in the ring toss, each joining one of the children while El and her dad pretended to referee. Though she and Rick still had their employment to deal with, they'd decided long ago that the old-fashioned rule needed to be challenged. If anyone could do it, she and Rick could. They'd already dealt with challenges greater than their employment. They both had talents and either one could work somewhere else if necessary. Laughter came through the back door and sounded sweet in Angie's ears.

Soon Rick ambled through the door and gave her a wink. Carly followed him, her face glowing with her secret, and Angie anticipated it was time for the announcement.

"Everyone." He motioned from the doorway. "Let's all go outside to the card tables and chairs so we can do our celebrating together." He gave her a grin and headed back out.

Angie heard Carly's giggles as she whispered to her daddy. Her smile reassured Angie that she had accepted her mother's engagement and her delay in returning home from Germany without being too upset. Rick had called her after he and Carly had talked to let her know how it had gone, and she was as proud of Carly as he had been and thrilled that they would go to Germany together on the honeymoon.

Honeymoon. Her pulsed skipped envisioning the real-

ity of her upcoming marriage and wonderful trip. Though taking a child along on a honeymoon might not be typical, she loved the idea. They would have a week or so following the wedding before they left and those private days would be enough before they left on the trip.

Her chest tightened as she watched their families and friends gather in the backyard. The roses were profuse, and the wave petunias had proved their worth by spreading into gorgeous displays of flowers. Today had been perfect.

Rick watched as everyone found a seat. The girls had chosen to sit on the porch edge, swinging their legs as they watched. Rick wandered in front of them and caught their attention. "Today we're celebrating Carly's sixth birthday, which means, in her words, she will go to real school in the fall. First grade."

Carly clapped her hands. "Kimmy and me are the same age today." She grinned at Kimmy.

Rick chuckled at Carly's preoccupation with her age.

He held up his hand. "But before we bring out the birthday cake, we have another event to add to our celebration." He beckoned to Angie, and she ambled to his side, her body tension evident as she stood near, anticipating, he assumed, the excitement he felt.

Curiosity had settled on everyone except Carly, who bounced nearby as if ready to jump into action.

"I imagine you're asking yourself what could be more important today than Carly's birthday." He grinned and gazed at Angie a second. "Nothing is the answer. Today is Carly's day, but she also wanted us to share another special announcement with you."

Carly shifted closer, her body as taut as an arrow stretched and ready for release. "Hurry up. I can't wait."

The crowd laughed, and he gave them a wink.

Angie appeared to hold her breath as he knelt on the grass beside her. Excitement sounded from those observing as he looked up at Angie, his heart in his throat.

"Angela Bursten, I have loved you forever though we know it's only been months. We began our relationship as coworkers and then good friends, and that's where love begins. Today I'm asking you to be my wife and Carly's second mother." He drew the ring from his pocket and held it suspended.

Angie's face glowed, and he spotted tears rimming her lashes. "You know my answer, Rick. You've made me happier than I've ever been. I love you with all my heart and Carly as if she were my own." The tears broke free and rolled down her cheeks.

She beckoned to Carly, who darted toward them with a prizewinning smile.

He rose and slipped the ring on Angie's finger.

Everyone hurried forward with hugs and kisses. Words of congratulations and best wishes flew through the air, and Carly stood close to them, her eyes glued to the beautiful diamond solitaire that would be joined on her wedding day with a band of smaller diamonds.

Carly tugged his pant leg. "Kiss Angie, Daddy." She bounced beside them, her gaze swinging from him to Angie.

While everyone chuckled and moved back to their chairs, he drew Angie into his arms and kissed her, their joy knotting together and flying heavenward. Angie had drawn closer to the Lord again on her own. He knew pressure wouldn't work. Loving the Lord had to come from her heart. The change added to his joy.

His happiness spilled over as Angie drew Carly into her arms and kissed her cheek. "I love you, Carly, with all my heart."

Carly's eyes spoke her emotion. "I love you, too."

Before the guests had quieted at their seats, the two mothers had disappeared without notice and returned with the birthday cake. They set it on a card table, and Carly skipped to their side while Angie's mom lit the candles and others broke into the "Happy Birthday" song.

"Make a wish, Carly." El's cheery voice matched his sparkling eyes.

Carly drew in a big breath and blew out the candles while everyone applauded.

Connie waved her hand. "Don't tell us what you wished for, Carly, or it won't come true."

Some adults shook their heads, disagreeing with Connie's childish response.

"But I want to tell." Carly's voice cut through the adults' murmurs.

His heart in his throat, Rick strode to her side and gave her a hug. "You can tell if you want."

Carly's face glowed. "I wished Daddy, Angie and I could be like a fairy-tale story and live happy every after."

Angie hiccuped a sob she hadn't managed to control, and his own emotion blurred his eyes as she joined them beside the cake. He clasped Angie's hand. "We couldn't have asked for a better wish, Carly."

Applause sounded, and Rick's world expanded, as he envisioned life with the woman he loved and the unexpected joy of having Angie as Carly's new stepmother.

The day couldn't have been more perfect. Glenda had called earlier and told Carly that she would take vacation time when Carly visited Germany so they could spend time together without interruption. Something wonderful had happened with Glenda. She'd changed and maybe it was finding love that made her life whole again.

Whatever it was, he lifted his eyes to heaven, thankful

for the amazing gift he'd been given. He slipped his arm around Angie and drew Carly to his side, his heart full. He'd had no idea the day he drove to Lilac Circle to help a friend move that his life would change forever. He glanced at the homes on each side of Angie's and wondered what life held in store for others who lived on Lilac Circle.

* * * * *

REQUEST YOUR FREE BOOKS!

2 FREE INSPIRATIONAL NOVELS
PLUS 2
FREE
MYSTERY GIFTS

Love Inspired®

YES! Please send me 2 FREE Love Inspired® novels and my 2 FREE mystery gifts (gifts are worth about $10). After receiving them, if I don't wish to receive any more books, I can return the shipping statement marked "cancel." If I don't cancel, I will receive 6 brand-new novels every month and be billed just $4.99 per book in the U.S. or $5.49 per book in Canada. That's a saving of at least 17% off the cover price. It's quite a bargain! Shipping and handling is just 50¢ per book in the U.S. and 75¢ per book in Canada.* I understand that accepting the 2 free books and gifts places me under no obligation to buy anything. I can always return a shipment and cancel at any time. Even if I never buy another book, the two free books and gifts are mine to keep forever.

105/305 IDN GH5P

Name	(PLEASE PRINT)

Address	Apt. #

City	State/Prov.	Zip/Postal Code

Signature (if under 18, a parent or guardian must sign)

Mail to the **Reader Service:**
IN U.S.A.: P.O. Box 1867, Buffalo, NY 14240-1867
IN CANADA: P.O. Box 609, Fort Erie, Ontario L2A 5X3

**Are you a subscriber to Love Inspired® books
and want to receive the larger-print edition?
Call 1-800-873-8635 or visit www.ReaderService.com.**

* Terms and prices subject to change without notice. Prices do not include applicable taxes. Sales tax applicable in N.Y. Canadian residents will be charged applicable taxes. Offer not valid in Quebec. This offer is limited to one order per household. Not valid for current subscribers to Love Inspired books. All orders subject to credit approval. Credit or debit balances in a customer's account(s) may be offset by any other outstanding balance owed by or to the customer. Please allow 4 to 6 weeks for delivery. Offer available while quantities last.

Your Privacy—The Reader Service is committed to protecting your privacy. Our Privacy Policy is available online at www.ReaderService.com or upon request from the Reader Service.

We make a portion of our mailing list available to reputable third parties that offer products we believe may interest you. If you prefer that we not exchange your name with third parties, or if you wish to clarify or modify your communication preferences, please visit us at www.ReaderService.com/consumerschoice or write to us at Reader Service Preference Service, P.O. Box 9062, Buffalo, NY 14240-9062. Include your complete name and address.

LI15

SPECIAL EXCERPT FROM

*Can an Amish widow inspire her patient to live...
and love again?*

*Read on for a sneak preview of
AN AMISH HARVEST, the first book in*
Patricia Davids*'s heartwarming new series*
***THE AMISH BACHELORS**.*

Samuel waited impatiently for his brother to adjust the pillows behind him. With his eyes covered by thick dressings, Samuel had to depend on his hearing to tell him what was going on around him. Maybe forever.

If he didn't regain his sight, his days as a master carver were over. He wouldn't be of any use in the fields. He wouldn't be much use to anyone.

"There. How's that?"

Samuel leaned back. It wasn't any better, but he didn't say that. It wasn't Luke's fault that he was still in pain and that his eyes felt like they were filled with dry sand. After six days, Samuel was sick and tired of being in bed, and no amount of pillow fluffing would change that, but he didn't feel like stumbling around in front of people looking hideous, either. Only his mouth had been left free of bandages.

"Is there anything else I can do for you? Do you want me to fluff the pillows under your hands?" Luke asked.

Before Samuel could answer, Luke pulled the support from beneath his right hand. Intense pain shot from Samuel's fingertips to his elbow.

LIEXP0615

"I'm so sorry. Did that hurt?"

Samuel panted and willed the agony to subside. "I don't need anything else."

"Are you sure?" Luke asked.

"I'm sure," Samuel snapped. He just wanted to be left alone. He wanted to see. He wanted to be whole. He wanted the pain to stop.

He caught the sound of hoofbeats outside his open bedroom.

"*Mamm* is back." The relief in Luke's voice was almost comical, except Samuel was far from laughing. He heard his brother's footsteps retreat across the room.

An itch formed in the middle of Samuel's back. With both hands swaddled in thick bandages, he couldn't reach to scratch it. "Luke, wait."

His brother's footsteps were already fading as he raced downstairs. Samuel tried to ignore the pricking sensation, but it only grew worse. "Luke! *Mamm!* Can someone come here?"

It seemed like an eternity, but he finally heard his mother's voice. "I'm here, Samuel, and I've brought someone to see you."

He groaned as he heard the stairs creak. The last thing he wanted was company. "I'm not up to having visitors."

"Then it's a pity I've come all this way." The woman's voice was low, musical and faintly amused. He had no idea who she was.

Don't miss
AN AMISH HARVEST by Patricia Davids,
available July 2015 wherever
Love Inspired® books and ebooks are sold.

Jonathon's eyes roamed Fanny's face, then her gown.
Appreciation filled his gaze. "You're wearing my favorite
color."

"I…know. I chose this dress specifically with you in
mind."

Too late, she realized how her admission sounded, as
if her sole purpose was to please him. She had not meant
to reveal so much of herself.

He took a step forward. "I'm flattered."

He took another step.

Fanny held steady, unmoving, anxious to see just how
close he would come to her.

He stopped his approach. For the span of three heart-
beats they stared into each other's eyes.

She sighed.

"Relax, Fanny. You've checked and rechecked every
item on your lists at least three times, probably more. Go
and spend a moment with your—"

"How do you know I checked and rechecked my lists
that often?"

"Because—" his expression softened "—I know you."

There was a look of such tenderness about him that

for a moment, a mere heartbeat, she ached for what they might have accomplished together, were they two different people. What they could have been to one another if past circumstances weren't entered into the equation.

"We're ready for tonight's ball, Fanny. *You're* ready."

She drew in a slow, slightly uneven breath. "I suppose you're right."

He took one more step. He stood so close now she could smell his scent, a pleasant mix of bergamot, masculine spice and…him.

Something unspoken hovered in the air between them, communicated in a language she should know, but couldn't quite comprehend.

"Go. Spend a few moments with your mother and father before the guests begin to arrive. I'll come get you, once I've changed my clothes."

"I'd like that." She'd very much enjoy the chance to show him off to her parents.

He leaned in closer. But then the sound of determined footsteps in the hallway caught their attention.

"That will be Mrs. Singletary," she said with a rush of air. The widow's purposeful gait was easy enough to decipher.

"No doubt you are correct." Jonathon's gaze locked on her, and that was *not* business in his eyes.

Something far more personal stared back at her. She had but one thought in response.

Oh, my.

Don't miss
THE MARRIAGE AGREEMENT by Renee Ryan,
available July 2015 wherever
Love Inspired® books and ebooks are sold.